Running in the Moonlight

Luxe Huntley

Published by Luxe Huntley, 2024.

RUNNING IN THE MOONLIGHT

First edition. May 1, 2024.

Copyright © 2024 Luxe Huntley.

ISBN: 979-8224398966

Written by Luxe Huntley.

for Matt

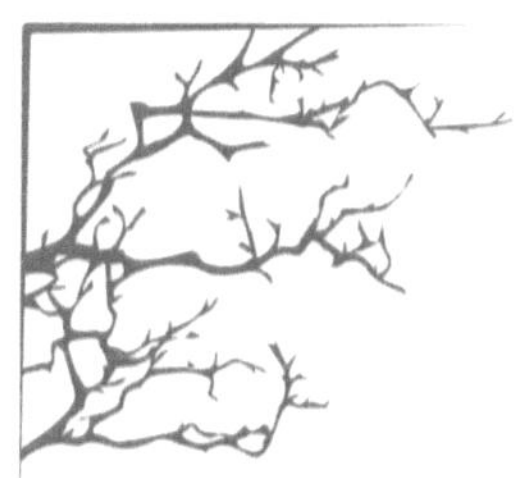

Chapter 1

When Lila left Emil's Hollywood mansion, she had only had half a plan. She realized that. It had seemed like a whole plan at the time but it was painfully clear now: merely half.

He found me so easily, she thought, as she raced back to the storage facility where she'd been hiding. He was on his way here, to this tiny high desert town she'd chosen randomly. The only miniscule upside to him having taken over her mind was that every once in a while she could see through his. And he was pulling off the freeway onto the road into town.

It was ten PM. Seven hours until dawn. She could realistically make it a hundred miles in that time. But really she had six hours because she would need time to find a crypt or basement to hide from the sun.

Lila slipped into the silent, hulking building. After eight there was no security guard, just a keypad. The hallways were filled with shadows cast by widely spaced fluorescent lights, flickering.

Her unit was deep inside the maze like rows of orange sliding doors. It was six feet by four feet of solid, comforting cinderblock and concrete floor.

Sliding her door up, she snatched up her fanny pack of Cash and fake IDs. She was back out before the door had rolled all the way up. Lila didn't bother sliding it back down.

She ran through the halls, heading for the back of the building. She needed to figure out a better way to hide her scent. That had to be how Emil had tracked her to this specific random town, a hundred miles northeast of his Mulholland Drive mansion.

The streets of this little high desert town were dusty, lit only by buzzing orange sodium street lamps. This area was made up of light industrial buildings, a car impound lot, some abandoned-looking warehouses.

Lila kept deep in the shadows of the buildings. As far as she knew, Emil hadn't found her lair. He only knew she was somewhere near here, but that wouldn't last long. His senses were so fine grained, so precise. It was possible he was toying with her even now.

Either way she needed to run. She would zig west, back towards the coast.

The storage warehouse was about a mile from the highway. There wasn't enough vegetation to bother finding cover on the sides of the road so she jogged lightly down the middle of the pavement.

This town was a lot like her hometown, Lawry. Dusty mailboxes in front of ramshackle farm houses. Chain link fences, to protect what? A rusted minnie winnie on blocks?

She shook her head and jogged faster.

As she was turning onto the state route, the scent of a dog drifted past. She slowed.

Emil hated dogs. If one came near the house when he was up, he would wrinkle his patrician nose dramatically as though he smelled shit. *Filthy creatures. Carrion eaters.* She could hear him sneering it.

Lila turned towards the scent. Maybe a stray dog wouldn't mind walking with her. She actually loved dogs. Vampires weren't supposed to, but she always had.

Such were the contradictions that were inherent to having lived longer as a human than she yet had as a blood sucker. Emil's humanity had drained away decades ago, but her soul was still clinging to her body.

"Hey buddy," she murmured sweetly when she caught up with the dog, who was loping along a farmer's fence a few hundred yards off the road.

The dog, a lean but well-cared for Malinois mix, glanced up at her. He flicked his ears in a gesture of welcome, but didn't stop. She matched his pace, following him along the fence.

Down a slight hill, the black-eared dog found what he'd been looking for: a dead deer. Lila crouched down and watched him sniff all around the carcass, pawing at the dirt near it.

The moon was a sliver but Lila didn't need light to see the canine's velvety, muscular form as he began to roll in the dirt around the deer carcass.

Presently, he had his fill and stood up. The dog shook himself and looked around as if to compose his thoughts. Lila slipped in front of him, and crouched down to look him in the face.

"Let me have your scent," Lila murmured, gazing into the hound's shining eyes. His tongue hung out and he gave her a friendly pant. She scritched his perky black ears and stood. He leaned against her as she pet him all over, rubbing her hands deep in his coat.

She let go and he wagged his tail.

"Thanks, buddy," she said. The dog dipped his head and ran off the way he'd come.

Lila could smell herself now. Deer carcass and stinky dog - better even than garlic for warding off vampires.

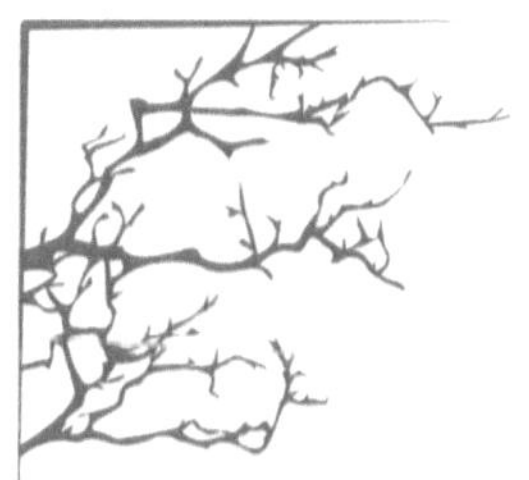

Chapter 2

Liam's eyes bulged in fear as Cash's fist drew back to hit him again. Blood already trickled from his nose and brow. Cash gripped the front of Liam's flannel and shook him. The urge to rip him to shreds was mounting, boiling, ready to spill out. Cash would make him pay.

Cash bared his teeth. Adrenaline surged through him, to power his killing blow.

BEEP BEEP BEEP BEEP BEEP

Cash rolled over and smacked his clock radio to shut off the strident alarm.

Another dream about his middle school bully. Liam seemed to represent all of the assholes that made his life hell for so long. Cash had no idea why Liam was his mind's choice. Others had done worse, and Liam pretty much left him alone after they got to high school.

Besides, no one was bullying him now. High school had been over for four years, and in the meantime he had gotten bigger and more confident. He wasn't a brute, but assholes like Liam steered clear.

Liam who still lived here too. He worked at a gas station. Nothing wrong with that. Maybe one day Cash would be the kind of Zen person who could forgive. Today was not that day.

Another early morning at a jobsite in San Simon. Luxury condo block. Cash was glad to be done for the day and headed home to Lawry.

He switched from traffic and weather over to the college station. His friend Carolina had a show at commute time. Cash listened every day. She played mostly post punk and dark wave which wasn't necessarily his thing, but he liked hearing what she liked.

Traffic crept along. The weather was finally starting to cool down. Longer nights, too.

His car stereo relayed a phone call. He tapped the answer button and eased off the brakes.

"Hi Spencer," he answered.

"Bro. I know you wake up early but you gotta come out with me tonight."

"Awww, Spence, come on."

"Buddy. I know. But this girl only wants to meet up in a group."

Cash sighed.

"Where, in Lawry?"

"Yeah. El Greco."

At least they have a good jukebox, Cash thought.

"What time?"

Showered and fresh, Cash put on clean black jeans and a Power Trip baseball tee. He ran hot, but he put on his usual leather jacket/ denim vest top layer. It felt like armor.

He checked himself in the closet door mirror. He needed a shave. Ugh, he needed to clean up his room too.

His hair was especially grandiose this evening. He buttered up his hands with curl cream and ran it over and through his hair, like his grandma taught him as a little boy. He even flipped his head over and worked the moisturizing cream through the underneath. That would have to do. Wash day was tomorrow.

Spencer had offered to drive but Cash declined. Spencer was as likely as not to go home with whomever his app date was, and it would be too awkward to ride back home in the back seat while his best friend tried not to acknowledge that he was getting laid. Plus, Cash lived way out on the western edge of town - it was totally out of the way.

Spence seemed to think Cash's perpetual datelessness was a big problem that he, Spencer, needed to assuage. Cash's opinion on the matter was apparently irrelevant.

Their mutual friends had often noted that Spencer and Cash were opposites and their love lives were merely one example. Cash was tall, half-Black, with a wide nose set in a sculpted face and an omnipresent five o'clock shadow. His spiral curls floated around his head like a lion's mane. His frame was lean but broad-shouldered, and he dressed like the metalhead electrician he was.

Spencer was none Black, average height, muscular, lighter complected than Cash with short dark hair he wore charmingly mussed. He was a bit baby faced, and still couldn't grow a beard at twenty three, like a perpetual choir boy. His cheerful smile and natural charm had always helped him slip past Lawry High's various bullies like a fox, while Cash was sullen enough to attract them and bullheaded enough to stay and fight.

Oh, and one other thing. Cash was a werewolf, and Spencer... wasn't.

They'd been best friends since kindergarten. Spring of senior year, Cash experienced his first transformation, in the passenger seat of Spencer's Barracuda on their way to pick up his Spring Fling date. The full moon hit Cash and his skin turned inside out, fur sprouting all over his body, fangs springing from his jaws.

Spencer spun an illegal u-turn and sped into the hills, away from town. He had no idea what was happening and was purely operating on instinct. When they reached the thick woods west of town, Cash leapt from the car before it had stopped, and tore his shredded clothes from his monstrous body. Half man, half wolf, but bigger than either. His glowing yellow eyes, Spencer later told him, were terrifying because they had such obvious human intelligence behind them - but no apparent human emotion.

"Hey man. Hey. It's me," Cash's best friend had cajoled him that night, and Cash remembered hearing him and coming back to his body. It was like he was operating an Abrams tank instead of the Toyota Corolla he was accustomed to.

"SSSsspppppeeeeennnnnncccerrrrrr," he slurred. His voice was gratingly inhuman, and somehow not animal either. The sound was like a computer talking through a fan. Both he and Spencer winced at it. "I hhhrrrrraaaaaffff toooooo rrrrrrrrrrrr." He tried to enunciate "run" but all he could do was growl when he tried to say it. Spencer nodded and shooed him.

"Go. I'll wait, dude."

Cash ran that night, ran so far and so fast. He had never been so alive, so full of sensations and blood and vigor. He took down a rabbit, its gore gushing down his throat. He howled madly, passionately. He could have fucked anything, he could have run for a thousand miles. His human body had never been so powerful, had never had such quiveringly alert senses and nerve endings.

As the moon began to set, his animal energy began to wane, and he found himself wanting to eat and rest. Without having to think about it, he found his way back to the pullout where Spencer had parked, trotting patiently on all fours.

How do I change back, he wondered, then tripped over his own now-human feet. *Oh.*

He stood up and looked at his human hands. No claws, just fingernails. No fur, just his natural hairiness.

"Bro, you're fully naked," Spencer had called, leaning out of the car. He rubbed his eyes sleepily. It was just after dawn. "Get in," he said, and started the engine.

Cash climbed in, holding his privates, his cheeks hot.

Spencer wordlessly reached into the back seat and pulled forward a quilt.

"I keep blankets in the car. Girls always get cold, bro."

After that, when they went back to school on Monday, Cash was changed. He stood taller. The jocks who made fun of his hair and clothes thought twice now. His human body wasn't that different but the person inside was.

The parking lot of El Greco was two thirds full. A busy night for a Wednesday. Cash showed the door gal his ID and headed inside.

At one point, someone had put a ton of work into decorating this place. The walls were deep red and featured dozens of framed velvet paintings. Silk flowers festooned the rafters, intertwined with red christmas lights. Electric chandeliers hung a few inches too low, casting feeble light on the sticky black and red booths. The floor was black and white checkers, and there was a nominal six inch high stage that Cash had never seen set up for a show. The bar itself was long and serpentine, with a red leather rail, and backed with a long gold mirror that made the liquor stock look much more plentiful.

Since that loving hand had relinquished control of the bar, it had settled into dinginess, a thick layer of greasy dust on all the paintings and even the little red bulbs of the Christmas lights. The jukebox was half Tejano, half classic rock.

It was the only bar in Lawry that Cash could stand.

"Cash! Over here dude," Spencer called to him. There they were, over in that cramped little corner booth. Cash's long legs would be sticking out in the walkway all night. Spencer and his date sat facing the door. She was Spencer's type, a petite shiny-haired brunette with a big cute smile. There were two other heads sitting opposite them. He steeled himself to walk over.

"Hey, man," they greeted each other, Spencer standing to clap Cash on the back.

"Anybody need a drink?" Cash asked, before Spencer could even introduce him.

"Yeah, I'll come with you.

"Dude, what's up?" Spencer asked the second Cash rested his forearms on the padded bar rail.

"I dunno man. It just makes me, like, antsy." They had to talk loud over "Conexion" by La Firma.

"What, talking to girls?"

"No, the whole pretending to be on a double date aspect."

"It's obviously not a double date, dude. It's just a group hang. Melissa's friends are cool."

"Sure. Hey, Bonnie, can I get a Bud and a Laphroaig. And whatever this asshole wants."

"We'll get another round of the same, Bon."

Bonnie moved off to get their drinks. A woman of very few words, Bonnie.

"It's fine, Spencer. I won't be weird."

"Bro, you're never weird, that's all in your head. Just have fun with us. Let's play pool."

Morgan, one of Melissa's two friends, flipped her long black curls behind her shoulder and leaned down to line up her shot. Cash stood at the end of the table, re-chalking his cue stick.

"So how do you know Spencer?" asked Ilena, Melissa's other friend.

"We go back to kindergarten," Cash smiled.

"Wow, really?" Ilena was a lot shorter than him, and she kept tugging him down so she could talk into his ear. And she kept pushing his hair away from his ear, her fingers brushing his earlobe or his cheek. He could hear fine with his hair in front of his ears. But he played along. What was the harm?

He wouldn't be acting on that pleasant sensation or her obvious flirting. She was very cute, they both were. That wasn't it at all.

Cash sipped his Scotch. The intensity of the flavor occupied his senses for the moment.

"Your turn Lena," Morgan sang, hopping onto the barstool closest to Cash.

He hoped they wouldn't hold it against him.

To no one's surprise, Cash wound up driving both Morgan and Ilena home, since Spencer had been their rides too, and he and Melissa had been pretty transparent about wanting to get back to his as quickly as possible.

Even though his truck had a back seat, they were all squished in the front. Morgan was in the middle, and her thigh was warm and soft against his.

Ilena's house was further away so he dropped her first. Morgan didn't scoot over.

Cash stilled himself. The moon was only three quarters, he still had control. He thought of the flavor of the smoky whisky on his tongue, the way it burned.

Radio turned up, he pulled into Morgan's driveway.

"I had a really good time tonight," she said lowly, her torso turned to him.

"It was nice meeting you," he replied, not returning her body language.

She said nothing for a moment. She was waiting for him to make a move. He kept his hands on the wheel.

"Well, see you around," she said, and he could practically hear her texting Ilena about his jerkiness.

He waved goodbye and waited for her to get inside, then threw it in reverse. His whole body relaxed, no longer tensed against the wildness in him that clawed to be free.

Cash pressed down on the accelerator. He rolled his window down and let the cold wind blow his long hair around. Before he could stop himself he was howling at the slit of the moon, howling along to Ozzy Osbourne on the radio.

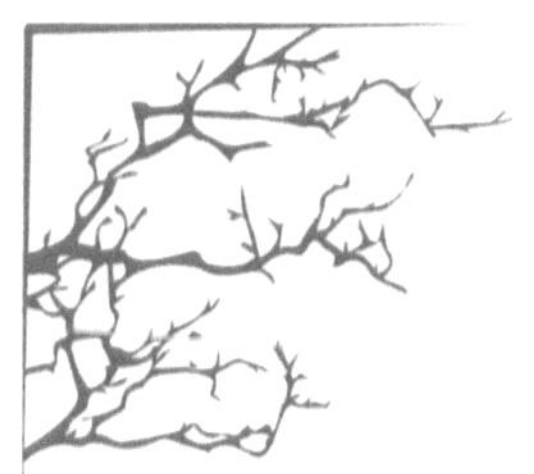

Chapter 3

Pale moonlight glazed the surfaces of the marble grave markers. The only sound, aside from bullfrogs in the nearby creek, was a low grinding as Lila slowly pushed open the marble lid of the crypt in which she'd hidden.

It shouldn't have been this heavy for her. She needed to feed.

Lila climbed down from the crypt and brushed the dust of bones off her. She smelled absolutely sickening - dead deer, dog, and now human bones and crypt dust.

She was closer to the coast now, where there were forests and hills that felt safer, more hidden. This cemetery was itself nestled in oak-dotted foothills. Finding a live human would be more difficult in this territory but that was the tradeoff of being safe from Emil.

She walked out of the cemetery and onto the town's main road. Everything was closed for the night. Not a soul was out, it seemed.

Side streets with Victorian houses next to small apartment buildings. It was incredibly quiet here. Real Mayberry situation. The people of this little town might not even come out after dark - she might have to move on to a place with more nightlife to feed.

Blocks away from the main street, heading north, she stumbled on just the right type of human. Her luck had held out for another night. A drunk, stumbling home from somewhere. She followed him for a hundred paces, and he never noticed her. So she sped up, sidling up next to him, matching his uneven strides.

"Hey honey," she murmured. Startled, he turned to her. His eyes were bleary. He could have been twenty five or forty five.

"Hey baby," he slurred.

"Want to go in the bushes with me?" she asked, putting a sultry tone in her voice.

He practically jumped at her. She took his hand and pulled him off the sidewalk, into a gap between houses.

He started groping her but she went straight for his neck, nipping his vein open with her fangs and drinking deeply. He moaned, too drunk and horny to realize he was in pain. Hot copper washed down her throat and she felt herself getting stronger, warmer, the life force filling and expanding in her. She kept drinking, draining, and soon she felt his hands growing weaker on her waist.

Gasping, she let go. Too close - he was pale and trembling. She gently deposited him on the grassy earth, and slipped away into the shadows. He would live and likely not remember anything - he would awaken with a pounding hangover, that's all. His blood, even with its nauseating sheen of alcohol, would keep Lila going for a few days. Not fair to him, but other vampires would have taken more, and she comforted herself with that fact. She might be a monster but she wasn't a murderer, not yet.

Picking up speed, Lila left this little village and went north, further from Emil and Los Angeles, closer to what she hoped would be safety.

She had never wanted this. Emil called it a gift. It was a curse. He and Sasha thought they were superior to the living, but since they had turned her, Lila was more dependent than ever on humans. The strength, the strange psychic abilities, the immortality - for some they were worth it. The four vampires Lila had lived with in Beverly Hills had, she was sure, been unbearable assholes when they were alive too. All they cared about was power over other people.

Lila had only been a bloodsucker for a few months. Thinking about the endless future ahead of her, it was too bleak. She kept moving, looking for a truck stop where she could pick up a ride.

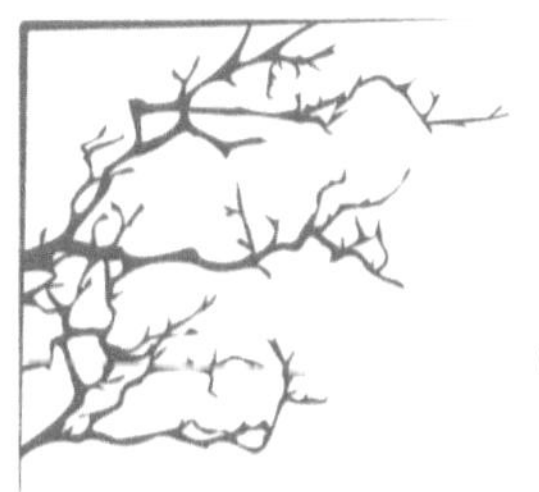

Chapter 4

"I just don't think any of that means you have to never date," Carolina said after her customary pause to think.

Cash sat across from her at the Golden West, eating a burger. Carolina dipped a fry in her milkshake.

"You wouldn't date me," Cash pointed out. He dipped one of his own fries in her shake.

"I will never understand why you don't order your own," she said haughtily. A long black nail pushed her acid green bangs out of her dark eyes. "Anyway, one woman not wanting to date you is not proof that you should cut your dick off. Wait, do you think it would just re-grow?" She tilted her head as though considering the implications.

"You're disgusting. But yes, it probably would. And it's not just one woman. I'll have you know several women have declined to date me." He took another bite of burger. He liked the Golden West because they made venison burgers. It helped, in between hunts.

"Oh what like Lila Phillips? The meanest girl anyone ever met? God, anyway that was years ago. You have changed MORE than a little."

Cash raised an eyebrow. Carolina rolled her eyes. The mention of Lila, even now, sent an icicle of heartbreak through him. He'd worked up his courage, waited for so long, and she had shot him down without a backwards glance. They never spoke again, and she'd left Lawry about a nanosecond after graduation.

"You realize you've never once lost control, right?" Carolina asked.

Cash shook his head.

"I just can't risk it. It feels... so close sometimes. Like my claws are just itching to come out. I don't know what would happen if I was with someone and lost it, you know?"

Carolina nodded and patted his hand.

"If I had any friends, I'd tell them to date you."

"You have tons of friends."

"You want to date my internet friends? The furries, you want one of those maybe? That would actually be perfect, wouldn't it?"

"Oh god, stop!" Cash laughed.

"Yeah I know just the girl. Well. puppygirl. Hey I bet she'd come to the show tonight, you want me to dm her?"

"Carolina. Please stop," he groaned. "I'm laughing too hard to eat."

"Oh how very dare I get between you and your true love, meat."

Cash rolled his eyes and shoved the rest of his burger in his mouth obnoxiously.

After dinner, they stopped at Spencer's apartment. He lived in a grungy little one bedroom in a neighborhood full of small apartment buildings. Spencer kept his place scrupulously clean.

"You two ready?" Carolina barked as they strode through the door.

"Hey, this is Melissa. Melissa, this is Carolina, she's like one of my oldest friends," Spencer attempted to introduce them. Carolina had already turned on her heel back out the door.

"She's in a hurry," Melissa commented without rancor.

The foursome piled into Carolina's Rav 4.

"Hey, Cash, how did it go with Morgan? Did you have fun?" Melissa asked, turning around to look into the back seat.

"Oh, yeah, for sure. Nice gal."

"Oh, but you didn't -"

"What should we listen to?" Carolina asked abruptly. She began to loudly scan through radio stations. "Classic rock? Country? Haven't heard this one in a while!"

Hank Williams twanged. Melissa looked confused but gave up.

"Cactus Club! Cactus Club! Punk rock music at the Cactus Club!" Spencer chanted, slapping his thighs in time. Cash and Carolina repeated the chant, then Carolina elbowed Melissa to get her to join.

Times like this Cash was so glad he had stayed in Lawry. He might not have a true pack, with his family being so far apart, but he had friends so tight they felt like family. And maybe someday, he would be strong enough to risk being close with someone.

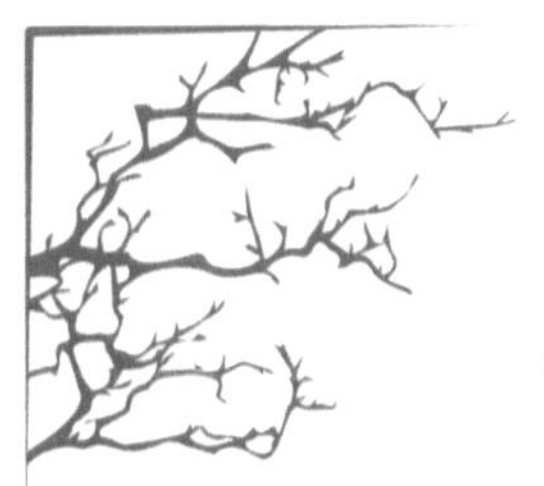

Chapter 5

The sun would be up soon and Lila still hadn't found a place to sleep. The semi she had been hitching a ride on had taken some unexpected turns. She had slipped off the back of it at what she thought, from the underside of the chassis, was a stoplight, only to find after the truck had moved on that she was in the middle of nowhere. Nothing around but redwoods and ferns, for miles up and down the winding highway.

I could have sworn we were in the central valley. But this feels like the Balenas mountains.

She was hungry, lost, and in danger of being incinerated by the sun. Normally she only had to feed every three or four days but she supposed she'd burned her last meal running from Palmdale to the interstate, where she'd found a truck to hitch on.

She stumbled off the pavement, climbing uphill and deeper into the forest.

The moon was nearly full. A memory of Sasha, Emil's mate, warning her to stay inside before the full moon, to avoid hunting at that time.

"It's almost as bad as being in the sun, honestly. It's horrid," Sasha drawled in her unplaceable accent.

Lila looked up between the trees, and the brightness of the moon hit her eyes. Immediate pain assaulted her retinas, like stabbing icicles. She looked back down, blinded momentarily.

Fucking fuck. I'm so bad at being a vampire.

Sasha and Emil had only taught her the minimum needed to survive in Los Angeles. They enjoyed watching her struggle. Like when she had tried eating a steak to quell the thirst and spent the entire following day writhing with cramps in her casket. They hadn't bothered to mention that human food was not only unappealing but indigestible.

Insects and birds were beginning to wake up and trill their little noises. Panic gripped Lila. Her mind raced trying to decide what to do.

There was a massive fallen tree just ahead of her.

Could I sleep inside that log? Would that work? No. It could have cracks. Fuck.

Frantic, Lila began digging under the log, like an animal. She flung mud and bark behind her, her hands like claws. The earth was soft and damp. She dug and dug until there was a hole big and deep enough for her.

Taking a deep but irrelevant breath, Lila climbed into the hole and began piling dirt in on top of herself.

It was harder than she expected to fill the hole from the bottom of it but at last she was sufficiently covered. Her hands patted the top of the dirt over her face and then retreated under the surface. She settled in for her slumber, hoping she was well and truly protected from the rising sun.

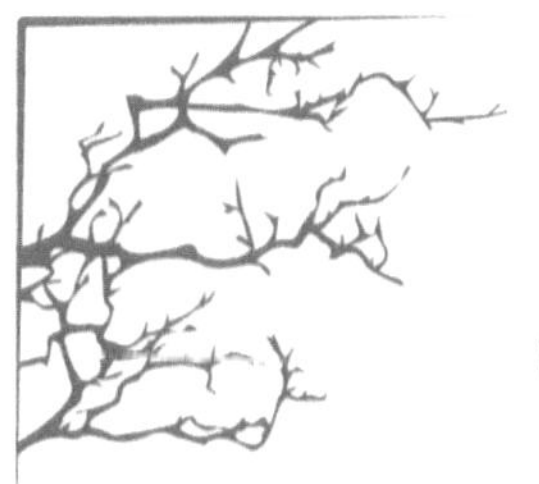

Chapter 6

It was the morning before the full moon and Cash was awake well before dawn. He was itchy with energy, the wolf in him clawing to come out. The previous full moon, it had been pouring rain, and not comfortable at all to run around in. Natural animals hid during rain storms and so did Cash. Tonight it was to be perfectly clear and crisp, the moon especially huge.

After Morgan brushing his ear the other night, the only female attention he'd let himself accept in a very long time, he was even more wound up.

Transforming on a controlled schedule made it easier to leash the animal part of him when he was in his human form. His family had taught him (once he admitted to his mom what was going on (and she confessed that she and his other relatives were also werewolves)) that animals had no ethics. If an animal could kill another animal, or take a potential mate, it had no ethical reason not to. But humans had a social contract, and compassion, and an evolutionary imperative to care for one another.

To live among humans meant checking his impulses. It meant not following animal rules, not taking what you could. It was just like his father had always said - might didn't make right.

Transforming burned off the flood of magic or hormones or moon energy. Whatever it was that caused "lycanism." No one in his family knew, or knew where he could find out. Much to his irritation.

A solid transformation, complete with running through the woods, hunting prey, howling at the mother of wolves in her shining fullness. That could buy him a month of satiated urges.

Plus, it felt fucking incredible. He craved it, sometimes, the feeling of power juicing through his veins in his beastly form. Every sensation turned up. Textures, scents, sounds, beautiful in their complexity that he couldn't see in his human form.

He hopped out of bed and put on gray sweats. He set a pot of coffee to start brewing in an hour, and sat on the floor with his toes under the couch.

A hundred sit ups and pushups later, he slipped his running shoes on and headed out the door shirtless to run in the misty early light. He bounced on his toes a few times to warm up, then jogged up his street and onto the state highway that ran into town.

Vineyards lined the highway, hypnotically lush lines of twisting green, heavy with late summer fruit. The air was redolent with hay and fertilizer. Cash loved living in the country. Growing things, wild things, all around. Air smelling of life, instead of burning petrochemicals.

He ran the three miles to the edge of the more populous part of town, then bore south to skirt the various subdivisions. Lawry had several state parks on its borders, which meant it could never sprawl out and encroach on the wilderness entirely.

Up through the southwestern hills, on human running trails paved and marked. Sweat began to trickle down his chest, wetting the hair down.

Eventually he completed a long loop. He filled his biggest mug with creamy, sweet coffee and sipped it while the shower heated up.

He put on the radio, and lathered up to the sounds of the college station's morning bluegrass show. The woody scent of his fancy body wash filled his nose, putting him in an even better mood.

His clean laundry was in a pile on his bed and he picked through it to find drawers and an undershirt.

This was not a tidy house. Laundry didn't get done promptly, mail piled up, and he had a ludicrous number of records and skateboards that he did not need. But he was clean, and he kept the house clean enough. No wolf wants to foul their den.

Some day he'd get around to tidying up a little.

Black jeans, black long sleeve, and black steel toes on, he poured the rest of the coffee pot in his thermos (black) and hopped in the car.

Cash checked his watch surreptitiously. The foreman had been going on about safety for fifteen minutes. It was Friday and a full moon - Cash had places to be.

"Okay idiots. Enjoy the weekend," Nilo dismissed them.

"Fuckin finally," Cash muttered, but there was no venom in it. His phone buzzed

"What are you up to tonight?" Spencer asked him.

"Oh, uh," Cash looked around to see if anyone was close enough to hear.

Before he could even open his mouth to say it though, Spencer clicked his tongue.

"Ah. Your thing. Your whole... moon thing," he hand-waved.

"Um. Yeah."

"Yeah okay. You better get going, I can practically hear your palms getting hairy," Spencer chuckled.

"Hilarious. Maybe tomorrow, bro. El Greco?"

"Yeah. For sure." They hung up.

Cash swung his dusty black denim - clad butt into the driver's seat of his black 1982 Chevy four by four. The jobsite was in San Simon, to the north, and his house was at the western edge. Even so, Lawry was so small it only took ten minutes to get to the little farm house Cash rented. When he was in high school, all he'd wanted was to leave Lawry. But life had happened and he had stayed, at least for now.

Lawry had its charms. It wasn't too far from Las Balenas, where his cousin Orion lived, there was a pool hall where he knew which tables were on a slant and which were level, there was a really good pho place. And of course Carolina, and Spencer.

Cash rolled down the main drag, First Street, patient with the Friday evening rush of cars. Strip malls, churches, and apartment buildings gave way to old Victorian houses, which gave way to empty lots.

Past that, where there were as many barns as houses, Cash turned off and cruised another quarter mile. His street, more of a gravel track, was also home to an equipment storage warehouse and the back gate of the adjacent goat farm. No other houses though. Just his little place with its huge fenceless yard, its carport, and its lack of neighbors for half a mile around.

Cash sat in his truck for twenty seconds after shutting it off, making sure no strange noises or smells awaited. Once he was satisfied he went inside.

He got a jar from the cabinet and stood at the sink, chugging water. Next he ate a banana and a bowl of Spaghetti Os. He washed his dishes and leaned on the counter, jiggling his leg.

He was practically itching to head out for his full moon run. He longed to race full speed through the forest, dodging trees, hunting prey. His claws and teeth wanted to come out.

When he pulled off his work boots and chucked them in the closet, the sun was finally starting to dip behind the mountains, dyeing the sky bright red.

"Fuckin YES," he grunted as he pulled his work shirt over his head. The build up of steam needed to be blown off.

Cash slipped into running shorts and headed out.

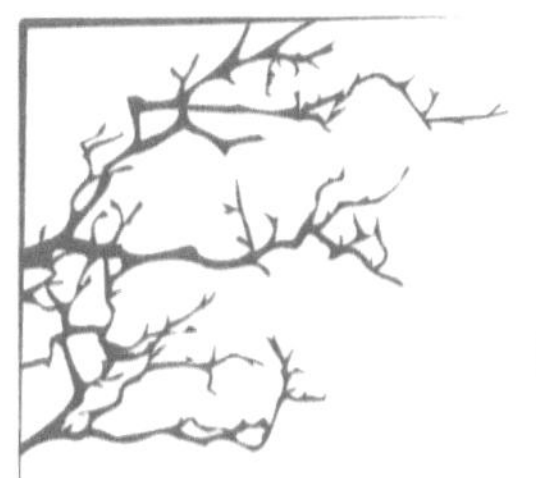

Chapter 7

The earth packed all around Lila had cooled, almost imperceptibly. That's how she knew it was safe to dig up out of her makeshift earthen grave.

Fresh cold night air hit her nose and she dragged herself up from the damp hole.

She crawled a few feet away, covering her tracks behind her, and waited in perfect silence. When she heard the insects, crickets or cicadas or whatever they were, start up again, she rose and began to slip silently from shadow to shadow.

Would have been a lot easier if the shadows weren't so sparse. Because Lila was truly cursed, it was now 48 hours since she had last fed, but she was as hungry as though it had been a week. Maybe when she had been confined to the mansion, she had needed less to stay alive. This hadn't been part of her calculations.

She had to eat tonight or she risked getting so hungry she went "feral," as the one who turned her had phrased it.

Thus, hunting was now or never. And of course, tonight was the full moon. The night when vampires are their weakest, the night when the moon reflects the most sunlight. Irritating her skin and eyes, making her weaker and slower.

On top of that, she'd only managed to make it to the Balenas mountains, outside Lawry. Her hometown. Unless she stumbled on a random camper she'd have to go into town to hunt. So there was a not-small probability of being seen by someone who actually knew her. She tallied how many people in Lawry had known her well enough to remember her.

Her family was long gone, having moved to Arizona right after she graduated. And she had never had much of a social circle in Lawry, not after ninth grade. But if she was going to run into anyone she knew, it would be in the one place outside LA where anyone knew who she was.

If - when - Emil and his minions trailed her here, it would be better if no one here had any information.

Plus, she'd never fed on someone who she knew. Emil had taught her to glamor victims, and it had always made them give her their blood willingly. Which in turn left them with the impression that she'd given them some undefinable, unknown gift, rather than having drained a considerable amount of their life force. This was all she had done to that drunk guy the other night. He would have woken up feeling physically bad but emotionally fulfilled and loved. But he had never met her, didn't know any different from the image she projected at him.

Someone who already knew her might be able to fend off the glamor more easily. There was so much she still didn't understand about being... this way.

Lila paused in a dense copse of redwoods. She was feeling something akin to the living sensation of lightheadedness. The forest around her bulged and retreated, the bright silvery light casting harsh shadows.

She listened. There, half a mile or so east - she could hear someone running. Jogging? The cadence was relaxed, but very fast for a human.

The trees melted around her, sliding past like figures in a crowd. Closer and closer, until she caught the scent, that delectable human perfume, so alive and rich and velvety.

There was another smell with it. Gamy, earthy. Was this person running with a dog? How could the dog possibly keep up? Not to mention, how was she going to catch someone running this fast?

It wasn't so long ago that Lila had been one of them but her humanity felt very far away right now. Her senses quivered around her, ultra sensitive like cats' whiskers, feeding her the intelligence she needed to make her attack.

Glamoring might be too slow, too sophisticated for her to manage in this state. She might have to simply pounce and hope fast didn't also mean strong.

There was the moon, pouring down as she entered a clearing no more than twenty yards from the source of the sound. It was coming straight towards her. She blinked away from the blinding brightness. It was another strike against her, the damnable moon confusing her vision.

She stumbled forward, aiming for the source of the sound.

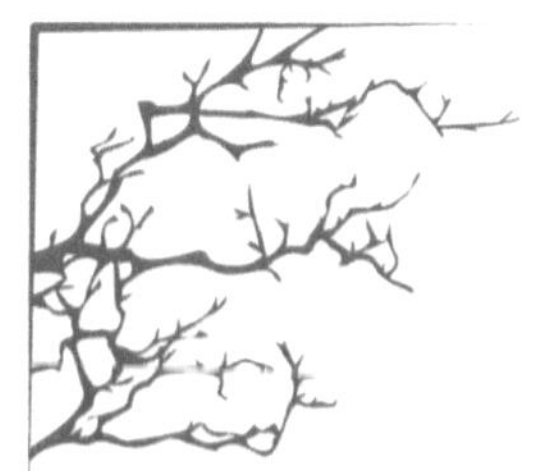

Chapter 8

Cash parked his truck at the trailhead and hopped out. The full light of the moon poured down on him and he shook himself all over, his umber curls flying. No other cars here. Not a sound of a human. This would be a good run.

The wilderness that had surrounded Lawry when he was a child had been steadily bitten away by housing developments, but there was still a substantial redwood forest covering the mountains between here and Las Balenas. This was where he would run tonight. He was only six miles from his house as the crow flew but the forest was so deep you felt a thousand miles from civilization. Just what he needed. His house was remote enough that he could sometimes get away with shifting at home and running in the farmland, but he felt much safer out here.

Cash stretched his legs and shoulders and scented the air. A wealth of odors greeted him. Earth, trees, rotting leaves, a trace of wood smoke. There was another note in the air, just a slender tendril of it, there and then gone. It was so familiar - maybe an exotic flower? - but he couldn't quite place it. Part of his mind kept turning that scent over, examining it.

It was good to warm up with a jog as a human, and then transform once he was deeper in the woods. It felt safer. If anyone saw him running in the middle of the night they wouldn't question it. At least not as much as they would if they saw a gigantic man-wolf.

Truck secured, he trotted into the mouth of the forest.

It was a cool night. Not a cloud in the sky. He was bathing in the moon's light, soaking it in. Half a mile from the trail head, he let his claws and fangs come out. His teeth grew in his mouth, so sharp they hurt to run his tongue over, and his hands became paws studded with daggers.

Sometimes just that was enough. Tonight though, he craved his full animal form. He wanted to run and run, to chase something down. His heart pounded for it.

Cash inhaled deeply over and over, picking up all the tiny molecules with his rapidly sharpening sense of smell.

He remembered the cacophony of scents that had assaulted him after his first transformation. At home, which then was the apartment he shared with his mom, it wasn't so bad. He slept almost that whole weekend anyway. But at school on Monday, everyone's BO was like reading their deepest thoughts. The smells at lunch made him want to hurl, the mixture of milk and hamburgers and mustard. He got a black coffee and stuck his nose in it the rest of the day.

His last period of the day had been art, which he had with Lila Philips. They shared a work table, in fact.

"What's with the coffee? Are you tired," she had asked flatly when he sat down with the cup, now cold, cradled close to his face. He pulled it away to answer but she was no longer paying attention. Her graceful fingers were at work on her painting, which he remembered was abstract, lots of black textures layered on each other.

That's when he smelled Lila's scent. She smelled clean, soft. A sweetness to her actual body odor, like all she ate was pineapple and avocado. Lila had always drawn his eye, with her dyed-black hair, her perpetual scowl, and her total disinterest in the social scene of Lawry High. But now her scent pulled at him like a siren's song.

It was shortly after that that he had screwed up his courage to ask for her number at lunch, and she had turned him down flat. He'd gone on a couple of dates that summer, and even lost his virginity with Sara Adubo. One night when he and Sara were making out in his truck, the hairs on the back of his neck stood up, and his claws started to slide out of his fingers. He had freaked out. He'd made an excuse to Sara about having to get up early and dropped her off. She had had to dump him because he was too cowardly to say it, and since then he hadn't dated sincerely at all. Four years.

Lost in this memory, two miles from his truck and well off the trail he got that scent, almost like blood but... dead. There was a wisp of that strange flower he had detected earlier, too.

His ears pricked up. He sucked in lungfuls of the night air, trying to figure out what that melange could be. Up ahead was a bit of a clearing, bright in the glow of the moonlight.

There, between the trees. A dark figure. They weren't moving. Was that even a person? Hunched low, face obscured. Barely visible.

It was definitely humanoid but its movements were not human - too fast, too silent, and yet jerky like a marionette. Cash kept running closer. Whatever this thing was, it didn't belong here.

The figure crouched down and Cash burst into the clearing. Their two bodies sprang towards each other.

His arm hooked across the figure's waist. The momentum whipped the figure off her feet and Cash dragged her (definitely a her-type shape under the filthy rags she was wearing) downwards, pinning her to the ground.

The creature fought like hell to free herself. That blood-flower scent enveloped her and invaded his nose. Familiar, enticing, yet a little gross.

"Stop squirming," Cash muttered, clamping his clawed hand around her wrist. She had long pointy nails, caked with dirt, and she was doing her damndest to scratch him anywhere she could. Her face was smeared with dirt and she had mud caked in her hair.

"Let me fucking go," the stranger spat, then lunged at his throat with her lips drawn up. He dodged at the last second.

"Are those fucking fangs? What are you?"

Her face was all dirty.

He straddled her and grabbed her wrists. How could this small human be this strong? She was putting up a really good fight.

Only once he had her limbs controlled could he look at her face.

Furious hazel eyes glared at him from a face smudged with dirt.

"*Lila?!*" he spluttered.

"Let me the fuck go!"

"Lila, what happened to you? Do you remember me?"

A hellish creaking growl escaped her throat and she flung her head up, slashing at his throat with her fangs. She missed, and shrieked in frustration. She bucked under him like she was possessed.

"Jesus christ!"

Cash tried to process what was happening. His high school crush, who had never given him the time of day, was sneaking around the woods all covered in dirt. And she smelled like death, and like flowers and none of her old honeysuckle musk, the musk must have been the scent of her life and now she was dead because... because she was a vampire.

Cash fought back the wild that was screaming to burst out of him. It didn't care that she was a vampire, it wanted *her-ness*.

When it was obvious he wasn't going to release her, Lila relaxed a little and stopped fighting.

"I'll tell you but you have to let me go. Or at least hold me at arms' length." Her voice was croaky.

He pushed back a bit, but kept his hands on her wrists. She relaxed a little more, but the strain in her jaw remained. As did the wild look in her eyes.

"So? What's going on?"

She lifted her upper lip in a sneer worthy of Elvis, revealing two long gleaming fangs where her canine teeth should have been.

"Are those real?"

"Yes, White Fang, I'm a vampire. I drink blood. I'm undead," she spat. The way she stared at his neck made his hackles raise.

Cash glared down at her. She slid her plump lips back down her fangs.

"Relax. I wasn't going to drain you all the way, just a little." He regarded her with a raised eyebrow. "So, how long have you been a wolfman or whatever?"

She swallowed. She was trying to play it cool but her restraint was tissue thin. She was squirming inside. He cocked his head at her.

"Your fucking claws and fangs, and oh, also, your eyes are yellow. Seriously though, can you give me a little more space?" Her eyes darted back down to Cash's neck and she licked her lips.

Startled, he extended his arms, hands still locked around her wrists.

"You want to bite me?" he asked.

She swallowed again. Like she was salivating.

"You're not afraid I'm gonna hurt you?"

"Well, are you?" Lila snapped. He made a face like he was considering it. "What were YOU doing out here, anyway? Did you know I was here?"

"What? No. I come out here every full moon."

Lila opened her mouth like she was going to say something snide, but instead she clenched her eyes shut like she was in pain, and her jaw trembled violently.

"Hey, whoa, buck up buttercup," Cash coaxed.

Her scent washed over him with her movement. Now that his adrenaline was down he could take it in fully, and he breathed deep through flared nostrils. He leaned a little closer and Lila huffed at him, her breath millimeters from his throat.

"Jesus christ. Are you, like, starving?"

"*Yes,*" Lila growled. Cash put her back at arm's length. His body was straining to transform. The moon was gushing down on him in all her might, and he hadn't switched for too long. And now this incredibly *female* creature under him, soft and curved....

He shook his head. The tips of his ears were itchy with newly grown fur, and his claws and fangs were still out, but he was pretty sure he could hold off his switch until he dealt with Lila.

"You're coming with me," Cash said firmly. Lila growled again in response. He dragged her up to standing and maneuvered her so she was in front of him.

"Where are you taking me?" she snapped, but didn't resist his hold.

"Somewhere you won't be a danger to anyone," he answered, and began frog marching her towards his truck.

"Let me guide you," he snapped the third time Lila tripped over a root. "Can't your kind see in the dark? You're a lot clumsier than I expected a vampire to be."

"It's not dark," Lila rasped. "The fucking moon is full. If it was actually dark you wouldn't have caught me."

Cash snorted. Soon they reached the trail head. Behind a massive sequoia, Cash peaked out at the parking lot. Still no other cars. He listened, scented the air. Nothing.

Gripping both of Lila's wrists in one of his massive paws, Cash got a bundle of zip ties from under the seat in his truck.

"Are you a kidnapper or something? Why do you have those?"

"I'm an electrician," Cash laughed. He bound Lila's wrists and ankles with the plastic ties and folded the front seat down.

Cash hoisted her up like a sack of potatoes and deposited her gently in the back seat of his truck's roomy cab. He shut the third and passenger doors and climbed into the driver's seat.

"Now don't you go biting my neck while I'm driving, Killer. I'm not gonna hurt you so you better restrain yourself."

"You got it," Lila muttered. Her voice was increasingly more demonic sounding, like she was crumbling in real time.

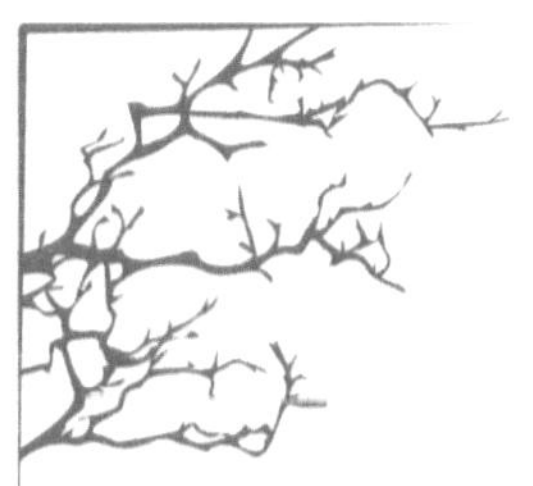

Chapter 9

He pulled his truck into the car port, really just an all weather tarp stretched between aluminum posts. Kept the sun and rain off his truck though. He hopped out and turned the headlights off. No sign of anyone nearby, no unusual scents or sounds. He picked Lila up around the waist and slung her over his shoulder. A continuous low, guttural moan came out of her.

He went straight through the kitchen and down the hall to the left, into his bedroom. His bed frame was high, the bed piled even higher with pillows and throw blankets. He flipped Lila off his shoulder and onto his bed, where she bounced slightly and then curled into the fetal position.

"Aw, fuck, I forgot you're all covered in dirt. Why are you so dirty?"

"I had to bury myself in the ground all day. I don't have my coffin with me."

Cash had to laugh. Lila glared at him.

"You seriously sleep in a coffin?"

"Can you turn off the light?"

He obliged.

"So can I just like, open up my wrist and pour you a nice refreshing glass of blood?"

Lila wrinkled her nose with distaste.

"Not you. Someone else could. A normal human."

"Oh well fuck me. Sorry I offered."

She sat up, drawing her knees to her chest and placing the circle of her arms around them. How on earth had she ended up at the mercy of a werewolf, THIS werewolf, who she had always thought was so cute and shy in high school.

"Don't be so sensitive. I can only have human blood. If I have werewolf blood I'll be, I dunno, double cursed. At least that's what the asshole who turned me said." She peered up at him, luminous hazel eyes through her thick dark lashes. "Starting to think maybe it would be worth it, though."

Cash, standing at the foot of his bed, stared down at her. His pulse was loud in his ears, his wolf half raging against the shackles he'd put it in. His teeth ached to take down something big, something she could share with him. He'd feed her, then take her...

Whoa. The wildness was screaming to be free.

"I have an idea."

He got his phone out of his pocket. Who could he trust with this? Carolina would never tell a soul but... she might honestly be a little too into feeding a vampire her own blood.

Spencer. Spencer was non judgemental and more importantly not busy. He had asked Cash what he was doing, so he definitely didn't have a date. And Spencer knew about Cash's own... affliction, so maybe he would accept the existence of vampires without a big fuss. Kind of like Cash just had.

Bro i can't explain over text but i need some blood.

Not thirty seconds later, Spencer texted back that he was on his way.

Lila lay on her side on Cash's bed. Her eyes were closed, and she had stopped trying to figure out how to twist off the zip ties. She was so tired, so weak. The full moon had drained her, leached her strength.

She didn't even have the vigor to puzzle out how in the hell Cash of all people had found her. He claimed he hadn't been looking for her but it was a one in a million coincidence.

How had she never realized he was a shifter?

That's why she shouldn't have come back to Lawry. Of course she would immediately come across someone who knew her. Now she was all tangled up, and there would be another person who could say they had seen her to Emil.

She should have headed some random direction, not towards the only other place she knew. That was just more proof of how toxic things had gotten in LA. Or maybe it was proof of what a big dumb idiot she was.

Lila was jerked out of her thoughts by the sound of the screen door being slapped open. She sat up and dangled her feet over the edge of the bed. She couldn't see the doorway from this angle but she heard Cash greet someone, and the two of them came down the hall towards her. Cash's tread was light, deliberate. His friend tramped like a stoned elephant.

"Spence, you remember Lila right?"

Spencer gawked at her. The veins in his neck might as well have been a neon sign. She struggled to hold in the panther scream of blood lust she had in her.

"Whoa. What are you doing back in Lawry?"

"Who are you?" she glowered at him. She might remember this dork but she wasn't going to let him know that.

"Spencer, you know, we had P.E. together -"

Lila looked to Cash in a way that communicated how much she wanted to know why the fuck Spencer was there. Was he parading delicious fat-veined idiots in front of her for any particular reason or just for laughs?

Lila had always pretended to ignore Cash, back in high school. Despite his metalhead appearance, he had seemed so sweet and gentle. She HAD to be mean to him, just to keep her distance.

Spencer on the other hand had been genuinely so annoying. He kissed her ass constantly no matter how many times she told him they weren't friends.

"Explain," she commanded.

"Okay so, Spence, Lila needs some blood. It's for... a ritual."

"Oh whoa, badass. So what are you gonna do? Are you gonna like, summon a demon or what?"

"Actually I'm going to drink it."

"Whoaaaa, for real?"

Lila stared at him without answering. Spencer shrugged. He was still a cute lunk head, the kind of boy a lot of other girls had been infatuated with. Puppy dog eyes, built body. He had absolutely no reason to ever be nice to anyone like her which is why she was so deeply suspicious when he was.

However, right now this glowing labrador of a human was grinning down at her and the veins in his neck were practically bulging with the vigor of healthy living. Lila smiled lazily. Spencer beamed.

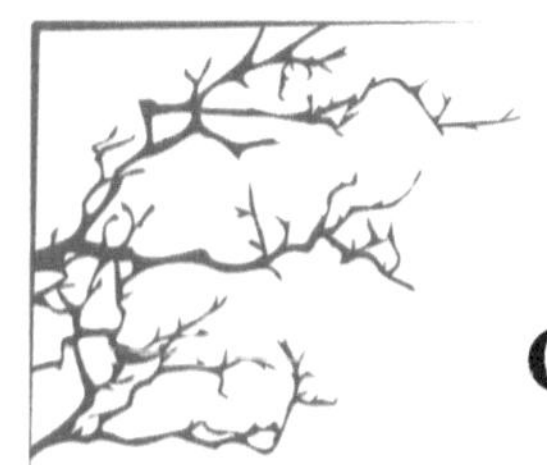

Chapter 10

"No, you can't take it straight from him, okay?" Cash whispered angrily. Spencer was in the kitchen downing Gatorade. She'd told him to replenish his electrolytes.

"I'll be so gentle. I'll be careful, I swear," Lila muttered back. Sounding at all human was a real effort right now.

"Yeah right. You're gonna go nuts as soon as you get your teeth in him."

"You don't know that," Lila retorted.

I do. Because that's what I wanna do to something right now.

"No. I'll have him put some in a jar, and you're gonna stay tied up until you've eaten."

"This is a terrible hotel. One star."

Cash rolled his eyes and left the bedroom, closing the door behind him.

Lila lay on her side across Cash's bed, and took in his room once again. Her thirst was hard to ignore, and it made her itch to thrash against her idiotic plastic restraints. She was so weak it wouldn't do any good.

In through the nose, count to four, out through the mouth. Her nerves buzzed slower. Cash's bed smelled like him, sweat and wood and ozone. His neck, his veins bulging, she couldn't get the sight of it out of her mind. Those teeth and yellow eyes.

This was not at all how this was supposed to go. She was going to feed on a stranger and move the fuck on from Lawry, maybe head up to the bay area.

"Alright, here it is," Cash bashed open the door. He had a mason jar half full of shimmering ichor. He was starting to look a little crazed himself, his wolf eyes glowing and his ears peeking through his curly hair.

Lila sat up and Cash held the jar to her lips. She grabbed it from him and drank. The hot liquid, fresh from Spencer's veins, gushed down her throat. Strength returned to her, pulsing through her the more she drank.

The jar drained, she licked her lips and licked the rim. Then she looked up at Cash.

His gaze bored into her, like he was trying to read her mind.

"Thanks," she said. She flexed her wrists and the zip ties snapped one after the other.

"Feel better?"

She nodded.

"Can I go now?"

He quirked an eyebrow. Spencer popped his head into the room.

"You good?" he asked. Lila hopped up and started to move towards him. The smell of the cut on his inner wrist, where he had sliced himself open for her, the scent of his blood was too strong. She had to have more. She had to take him, drain him. She had to -

"Alright thanks a bunch Spence! Let me show you out," Cash said too loudly. He shoved Lila back down on the bed and then pushed Spencer out of the bedroom, slamming the door behind him. Their voices moved down the short hallway and then Spencer's car started.

Lila stretched, and popped her ankle restraints off. The life force filled her, plumped her own veins, and the madness of the thirst subsided. It wouldn't be back for a few days. She was sated and glowing.

However, she was still filthy, loam under her nails and in the roots of her hair. Her clothes, all she'd been able to take with her when she left the storage facility, were caked with dirt. Her wad of cash was still pinned in her jeans pocket, she'd made sure of that.

This whole situation was utterly humiliating. Sleeping underground, hiding from the sun and the humans. Having to drink from a jar like a cat lapping milk.

Stupid, so stupid.

Cash came back.

"Look, I can't let you go."

She stared at him.

"What are you talking about?"

"Aren't you just going to find someone to... eat tomorrow night? I can't let you wander around Lawry murdering people."

"Well then you'll be pleased to learn that I won't need to eat again for a few nights and I was planning to leave town. I shouldn't have even come here."

"Leave tomorrow night." He waited. She waited.

He might think he could stop her but she doubted it. Now that she'd eaten, the superhuman strength she'd been promised had returned. On the other hand, she could use a safe place to regroup and think of a plan, a way out.

"You can stay here, get cleaned up, we'll figure out some sort of sunproof setup. It's almost dawn anyway."

She closed her eyes and sighed deeply. Maybe this was for the best. There was no chance whatsoever they would think to look for her here. She would just have to trust that Cash actually wanted to help and wouldn't open the curtains midday on her.

"Fine. I leave tomorrow night."

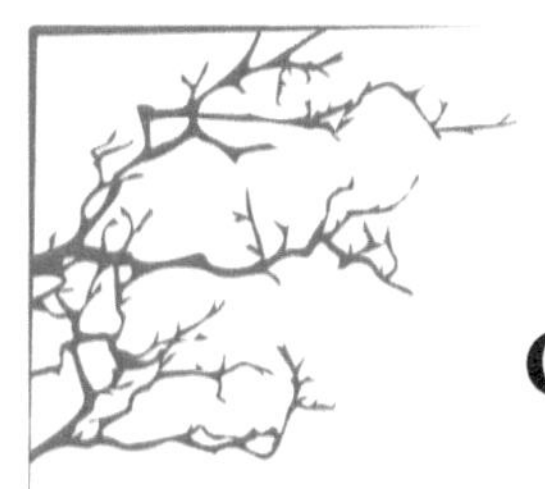

Chapter 11

Cash showed Lila the bathroom and left her to get cleaned up. Meanwhile he paced through his house, trying to figure out how to cobble together a coffin.

The house had one bedroom, one bathroom, and a kitchen-living room. Nothing in the kitchen or living room would suffice. There were no nooks or closets and the east-facing sliding glass door on the living room would be way too hard to black out.

The bathroom was out, because if he needed it during the day he would let the light in.

It would have to be in his bedroom.

He surveyed his room. It was a mess. Clothes piled up in the hamper, clutter on every surface, his closet overflowing with anything he didn't know what to do with.

The closet might work though. If he pulled everything out and put it... somewhere, the floor would be just long enough for a little thing like Lila to lie down. He could tack a blanket over the window.

The shower turned off. Cash started shoveling stuff out of his closet. What even was this junk? A wad of old phone chargers. A Spongebob beach towel. Old skateboard trucks. Old work gloves.

He groaned at himself. The one time a girl comes over and not only is she sleeping in his closet and not his bed, but she's also going to find out how messy he is.

"Hey Cash?"

He hopped up from his crouch and tried not to go running towards her voice.

"Yeah?" he asked with all the casualness he could muster.

"Do you have any like... clothes I could borrow?"

Cash blinked. Lila was NAKED, in his house. Of course he knew she would shower naked but being confronted with that fact so directly made his head spin. He shook himself hard, trying to get his wild nature under control.

"It's just that my stuff is all muddy," Lila added.

"Yeah, sorry, one sec."

Fuck! What did he have that was clean? He rifled through his laundry pile and found some sweat shorts and an old Cramps tee shirt. Did she need undies? That seemed a little intrusive but then would it be weird not to offer drawers? He decided to include boxer briefs and socks.

Lila cracked the bathroom door when he knocked. He stuck the clothes through and she took them like an eel snatching an anchovy.

Cash's clothes were much too big. They swallowed Lila entirely. Cash had always been taller than her but adulthood had made his shoulders and chest broad too. And, from what she had just glimpsed through the door, he'd grown a delicious dusting of dark hair across that broad chest and down his stomach.

Fucking hell. Was being full making her horny or something? She'd never thought of Cash quite this way before.

Kind of gross since he was apparently half animal. Or at least, Emil would have said it was disgusting. She wasn't at all sure it was gross and in fact his ears and fangs were kind of... cute. Like a kid in a Halloween costume. But not a kid at all, tall and strong, and with glittering eyes that glowed in the moonlight.

His tee shirt smelled a little like him, even though it was clean. It smelled like him and detergent. She pulled it over her head and looked in the mirror. The head of the lady on the cover art was as big as her own real, three dimensional head.

The sweat shorts were never going to stay up, nor would the socks. She slipped into the boxer briefs, and clipped her fanny pack on. It was oddly intimate, wearing Cash's underwear. She'd always kept him at a distance in school and here she was in his house.

Which made her wonder again why Cash was helping her. It couldn't just be the obvious answer - that he wanted to sleep with her. Harboring a vampire was significantly more danger than most people cared to put themselves in. Even a weak, hungry vampire, like she had been earlier. And even a shifter like him.

Emil had told her that vampires should never mix with werewolves. Their blood would make her double-cursed with all the weaknesses of both kinds, and their scent on her would make other vampires want to kill her. She didn't know what would happen to a werewolf that bit a vampire. Probably the same thing. Their packs probably tore them to shreds.

Maybe he wasn't afraid of her because he thought he was stronger or faster.

At sundown she wouldn't have to wonder anymore, because she was leaving.

Sufficiently clean and dressed, Lila emerged from the tiny bathroom.

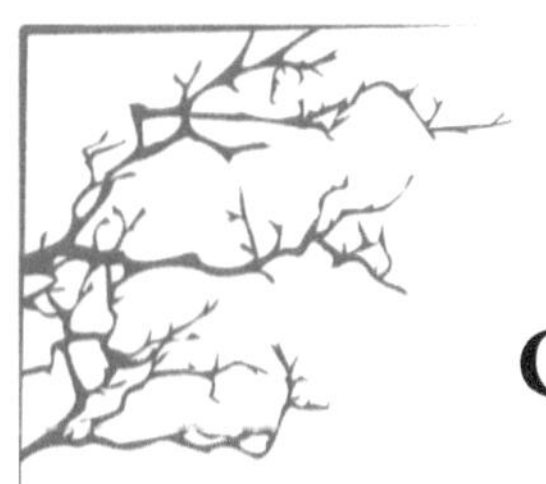

Chapter 12

Cash shoved the pile from the closet under his bed, and stood up to see Lila standing in his bedroom doorway.

He gulped. Lila looked exactly like she had as an eighteen year old delinquent. Her long dark waves hung over her pale shoulders, framing her heart-shaped face and almond hazel eyes. Her skin glistened from the shower. His boxer briefs clung to her legs and hips. He pushed his hair off his face.

"Um. So I cleaned out my closet. I think it should work. I'll hang a blanket over the window too.

Lila nodded.

"I can put a sleeping bag down and like, some pillows. Is that okay?"

"For sure. Listen you're not, like, trapping me here and then in the middle of the day you'll fling the windows open and burn me alive, are you?"

Cash's eyes widened.

"It's just I don't know why you would help me. Like are you just such a good guy?"

She was too tired and keyed up to be subtle.

"I guess so," Cash said drily. "I'm such a good guy."

Lila quirked up a brow.

"I'm not really helping you. I'm keeping you from killing anyone."

"I don't kill people."

"Oh, because you're such a good guy right?" His eyes glimmered. Hers rolled.

He pulled a sleeping bag down from the top shelf of the closet and unfurled it. Then he tossed a couple of pillows down.

"Your suite, m'lady," he said sarcastically, gesturing at the makeshift bed like a maitre d.

"Thanks," Lila said flatly. She got in the closet and slid the door shut.

There was no way she could see to secure the sliding doors from the inside. Lila pulled a bunch of clothes off hangers, and crawled into the sleeping bag, dragging the clothes and pillows behind her to block off the opening of the bag. It wasn't quite the velvet-lined coffin in the basement of Emil's Laurel Canyon mansion but it was a lot more comfortable than a hole in the dirt.

Cash stared at the closed closet doors for a moment.

He needed to shift tonight or he'd be a reckless asshole tomorrow. And he had to go soon. It was still before dawn, and it being Saturday meant people wouldn't be out so early. But the timing was awful. He'd only be able to run for a couple of hours. He'd probably need to shift again tonight.

Which wasn't a terrible thing. He liked shifting. There was no other feeling like it, no drug or sexual experience or thrill that could compare. But he also had to do it or he would cause himself a lot of problems.

He had to do it now, here at home. And run out his own front door in wolf form. It was so risky. Fuck it, he thought, and slipped out of his bedroom, shutting the door behind him.

In the living room, he stripped naked, and without making a fuss about it, let the wild wash over and through him. His flesh rippled, swelled, his bones crackled as they reshaped. Smells and sounds amplified and his vision changed - the colors softened and washed out while everything grew sharp, and grays took on the significance of colors.

Sensations slowed down, too, like he could process sensory information faster. In human form Cash puzzled over how to describe this often. There was no human equivalent.

He breathed deep into his lungs, the oxygen charging his fast twitch muscles. This part felt to him like the pump he got at the gym, but times a million.

Fur sheathed his body and he shook, settling his fresh skin and fur, and then shook again for the pleasure of it. He dropped to all fours, stretching and flexing his mitt-sized paws.

His cousin Carter shifted into a black wolf, more lean and tall. Carter's sister Orion became black and silver, thicker of frame just as her human form was built. Cash was the runt, a little shorter than Carter and leaner than Orion. He was tawny and black.

He didn't know any other shifters than his family - his pack - but he knew they existed. His mother and aunt talked about other packs and lone shifters.

Cash swiped open the sliding glass door that led to his back stoop. He sniffed the air and resisted the urge to howl.

On silent feet, he ran out into the night.

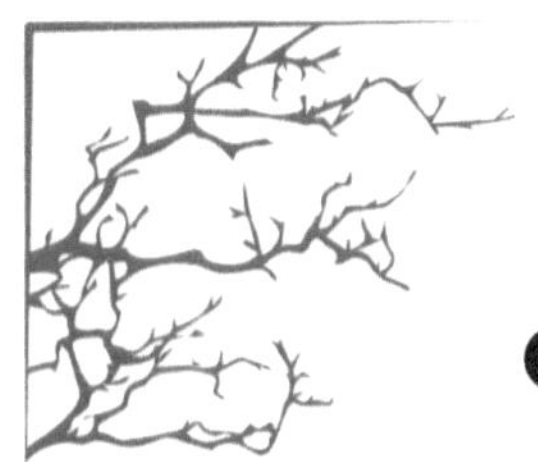

Chapter 13

One index finger poked a teensy hole in the wad of clothes Lila had stuffed between herself and the opening of the sleeping bag. She waited. No horrible burning. It was at least dark in the closet.

She pushed the shirts and sweaters out of her way. Why did Cash own this many sweaters?

It was pleasantly lightless in the closet. She sat up. Her shoulders dropped away from her ears for the first time since she'd left the mansion. Probably long before that.

Whatever Cash's plan was, he must not want to kill her. Part of her was idly curious what he wanted. Most of her, the smart, rational, self-preserving part, wanted to get the fuck out of this stupid little town as soon as possible. The faster she got out of here the further she could get from Emil and his little gang of psychos.

Lila didn't know what they would do if they found her. They might want to kill her. Or just make her go back. Either was unthinkable.

So it was really safest for her to go, tonight, right now. Safest for her, and for Cash. She was putting him in their warpath just by being here. She had been too feral last night to think about it, but Cash didn't deserve to be mixed up with Emil.

She still couldn't tell if the closet door was sealed well, or if it was actually night. The closet doors felt a bit too warm for full night.

"Cash!" she called. "Is it night time?"

He didn't answer. Maybe he wasn't even here. Maybe she would slide the closet door open and there would be a bunch of werewolves there to kill her. Anything could happen at this point.

She slid the door open a millimeter and stuck her pinky across the gap. No burn.

"Cash?" Was that snoring she heard? She checked his bed, even though she could see he wasn't in it from across the room.

This bedroom was tiny. It was kind of cozy, but the clutter was overwhelming. She didn't know how he could sleep at night with all this stuff staring at him. To be fair he had dragged a bunch of things out of his closet, but that was only a fraction of the chaos.

It was difficult to pick out any one thing. His bed was piled with blankets, pillows, and clothes. His walls were plastered with posters, photos, drawings. The top of his dresser had a menagerie of knick knacks and keepsakes, change, keys, pens, charger cords, screwdrivers, pliers, little metal items she couldn't identify.

Under the piles, his bed was actually neatly made.

"Huh, go figure."

He wasn't in the bathroom.

"Cash?" She came into the living room, where the sliding glass door was wide open. The heat was blasting - that explained why it didn't feel like night in here.

There was his hairy leg flung over the back of the velvety gray couch. All of Cash's furniture was oversized and cushy.

I should just leave. I should take some clothes and the sleeping bag and leave him a note and take off. Come on Lila. Do it. Go.

She went around the couch to wake him up.

He was sprawled out, buck naked, blood drying on his face and chest. Animal blood. It didn't smell great but the sight of it inflamed her thirst. Her eyes raked over him, taking in his thick chest, lean torso -

His fangs and claws were gone. So he was always this hairy.

Lila realized a nanosecond too late that her body was flinging itself onto Cash, her teeth bared at his naked throat.

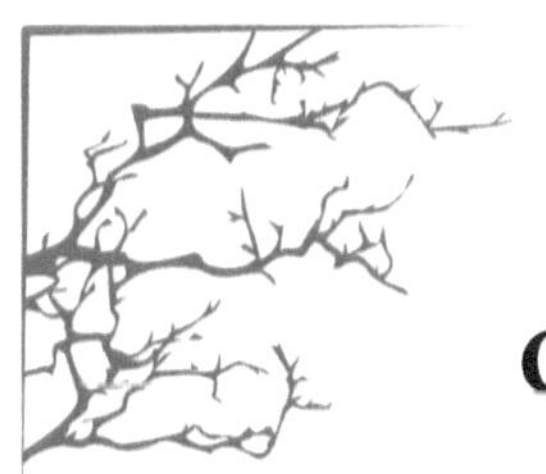

Chapter 14

Cash woke with a start and grabbed her, his eyes lit as if from within. His hands, still huge in human form, circled her waist and dragged her on top of him.

Lila snatched at his long curls and held his head still, no longer in control of her own movements. She hissed, and her fangs grazed the stubbled skin of his throat.

He jerked her back like he was waking up again, and Lila scrabbled to get up, seizing her faculties once more.

He was still holding onto her and then let go with a startled shove, and scooted up into a sitting position. She righted herself and then shook her head, trying to clear the bloodlust.

"Fuck I'm sorry I -" Lila started, and then glanced down to see Cash had the kind of erection they write songs about. Lila snorted. Cash flushed in embarrassment but his eyes were still lit up like Christmas. He grabbed a plush blanket off the back of the couch and covered himself.

"You're soaked in deer blood," Lila said. "I think it made me a little unhinged there for a sec. What's your excuse."

"Morning wood," Cash growled. He stretched and scrubbed his stubble, flaking blood off as he did so.

"Fuck," he grunted. "What time is it?"

"Night time. Listen, I was wondering if I could take some clothes and that sleeping bag. I'll pay you back eventually, I just, I really gotta get out of here."

"What's the big rush?"

She sighed.

"I don't want to talk about it."

"Well, do you have a safe place wherever it is you're going tonight?"

Lila pressed her lips together and said nothing. Cash looked her over, thinking.

"Stay another night. The closet was good, right?" He rubbed his eyes and stretched again. She studiously avoided looking at his treasure trail as he did. It was tempting to stay. The closet had been pretty comfortable, definitely better than bunking with a skeleton. But the longer she stayed the more danger Cash was in.

"That's not a good idea. I need to leave."

He held her gaze. Could shifters read minds? Lila had no idea.

"I need a shower. Can you at least wait that long?"

Cash cranked the shower to hot and brushed his teeth while the ancient water heater bestirred itself to produce.

He stepped into the stall and slid the glass door shut. The dried blood began to wash down the drain. He lathered his body as the steam filled the room.

The animal in him had taken over for a second back there. Sure, he was half asleep, and coming down from an intense shift. It wasn't great to lose it like that, though. He was a hair's breadth from flipping Lila under him and....

She did something to him. Always had. But when he'd been a kid, before he started shifting, he didn't feel like he was going to lose control. He should shift again, tonight. Maybe that would help.

He was an idiot, though, and instead of running again, he was taking Lila north. He was such a sucker.

Sometimes women who knew him now called him out for being so cold and aloof. He knew he came across like a jerk, because most of the time he didn't know how to rebuff their attention without being rude.

Little did they know what a big soft baby he was in reality. Lila wouldn't be any more interested now than she was back then. But he wanted to help her. And the wild part of him wanted to protect her, feed her, and keep her here forever.

In high school, sometimes they had detention together after school, sitting for what felt like an eternity in a beige classroom. They weren't allowed to talk but when the teacher wasn't in the room he would watch her. There was something about her that he couldn't ignore. She doodled in her spiral bound notebook, her only medium a black ballpoint pen. Drawings of dark stars, vortexes, galaxies, graveyards. He would make up reasons to walk past her desk.

Now she was here, so vulnerable in this form, and he could help her and take care of her, the way he couldn't before. The way no one had for her.

His morning wood was back. Cash slicked his own hand, and pretended it was hers.

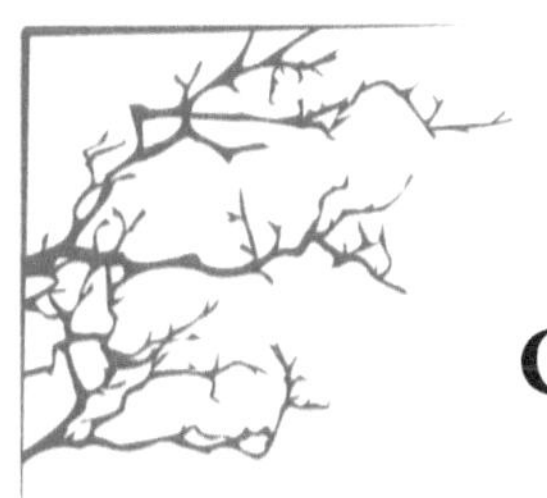

Chapter 15

Lila sat on the couch waiting for Cash. It was probably ten pm. If he was going to drive her, they could easily make it to San Francisco before dawn. Then she'd have to find a basement or mausoleum to break into.

She should probably feel guilty that Cash was going to spend his Saturday night chauffeuring her, and that she had no intention of ever speaking to him again.

It was for his own safety, though. The less he knew about her plans and whereabouts the better.

She heard the shower shut off. Her eyes closed, and she rested her head on the back of the couch.

It wasn't just Emil who Cash needed to be safe from. It was hard to resist those thick, luscious veins in his neck. Since he'd shifted to and fro, he was flush and full, his life force pumping through him. She had been so very close to sinking her aching fangs into him earlier.

He had no idea how close. Based on his offer to make sure she "got there safe," he didn't seem to understand what she was capable of.

Why else would anyone choose this horrible lifeless existence, if not to gain extreme power? Not that she had chosen it, she reminded herself bitterly.

The bathroom door opened. She looked behind her.

"Just be a minute," Cash called as he padded into his bedroom. His lats rippled under his deep taupe skin. She tongued her fangs.

Emil and Sasha had told her that the young, the athletic, and the powerful were the most sought after victims. When Lila had fed before it had been on young, dumb guys she picked up in bars in Hollywood. She never finished them off, not once. She took as little as she could even though the rest of the brood made fun of her mercilessly over it. They called her vegetarian, wet nurse, cry baby.

Those guys she drank from. She tried to make them feel like they'd enjoyed it. The first one, the glamor almost didn't work, and she was afraid she'd have to kill him or bash him senseless. But then, his cow eyes softened and he went all horny at her.

"Alright, ready, Killer?"

She hauled herself up, rolling her eyes.

Cash had packed her a kit: a change of clothes, a sleeping bag, a black canvas tarp, and a roll of gaffer's tape. And he had accepted without more questions that she needed to move on.

Asking why the fuck he was being so helpful seemed rude. For once, Lila kept her acid tongue to herself and accepted. They got in the truck. Lila closed her eyes.

"Sleepy?" Cash asked.

"The headlights are too bright," she answered. "I'll get used to it eventually."

The truck bounced down the gravel road towards the highway through town.

They drove in silence for a while, heading for the northbound freeway. Lila wondered if Cash had always been a werewolf. How could she have not noticed back in school? Back then he had been so skinny, so quiet. She could always see his gold-flecked curls from across the crowd, his thick brow raised at something dumb Spencer was saying.

Like her, he was always in trouble. Seeing him get dragged to the principal's office at lunch was almost welcome, because it meant he'd be in detention too, soon enough.

"What does it feel like?" Cash asked, breaking the hush of the truck's interior.

"What does what feel like?" She scooted up, adjusting herself to settle deeper into the leather seat.

"When you drink blood."

She paused to consider.

"It's like... if you could drink coffee, tequila, cocaine, and heroin all in one drink, and it also gave you superpowers."

He snorted.

"So, it gives you energy?"

"Kind of, but more. It makes it like... like I can feel everything, I can sense everything. Nothing can hurt me, and everything feels so good."

"How much do you have to drink?"

He accelerated onto the freeway, the engine roaring.

"Not that much. Maybe four ounces to keep me going."

"And without it you die?"

"Eventually. First I would basically go crazy from the thirst."

Cash nodded. Like he understood. Lila fell silent. Cash switched on the radio. The local college station.

"This is Carolina Skeletina and you're listening to KRKC. Next up, the Cramps with 'I Was a Teenage Werewolf.'"

Cash snorted.

Lila felt herself relaxing. It was like before, before she'd run away to Los Angeles and met Sasha. When she would ride around town in the passenger seats of guys' cars, listening to music, stopping to smoke cigarettes in the woods.

She felt... safe. Even though she knew Cash would be no protection against Emil, even though she knew they were both anything but safe. Cash, at least, would never hurt her, and that alone made her safer with him than with anyone else she knew.

Cash chewed his lip as he drove, one hand on the steering wheel. Red and white lights from other cars smeared past. He had to let Lila go, he knew that. She wanted to leave Lawry, she hadn't said why exactly but he figured probably because Lawry sucked.

It would be insane to just keep driving. To just go with her, keep running, pair off with her and run forever. He hadn't spoken to her in four years and they had barely known each other in school. Talk about coming on too strong.

This was just his loneliness getting the best of him. Since his mom and aunt, the last of his family, had moved away, he was at loose ends. Tying it all together with a mate would have been ideal. But it was deluded to pin that hope on Lila. On top of all the normal, natural reasons it wouldn't work there was also the fact that she was an undead bloodsucker. He didn't want to hold it against her but it was hard not to.

He merged from 101 to 85, the speedometer climbing. The southern suburbs of Silicon Valley zipped past behind concrete brick sound walls. Carolina's voice on the radio was comforting. She was spinning punk classics like the Damned tonight.

"Cash, you're a good person," Lila said. He glanced over. Her reflection was white on the black window.

"What do you mean?" he asked, turning the radio down. The lights of downtown San Simon rose ahead.

"You just are. You were nice to people in school. You're helping me now, for no good reason at all. I know I wasn't that friendly to you when we were in high school. I just... I hope you know you're a good person. Most people aren't."

"Um, thanks."

How to tell her that he was helping her for entirely selfish reasons? Even if she was a vampire, part of him still saw her as the unattainable goddess of his teenage imagination. He wanted to be near her. And he couldn't let her hitchhike to San Francisco and get into lord knew what trouble on the way when he had a perfectly good car and.

He merged and headed for the fast lane. Lila made a little noise, like a whimper.

"Are you okay?"

She was hunched over, her hands over her ears, rocking. She whimpered again.

"Lila! What's happening?"

"Turn around," she spat. "He's in San Francisco. Turn around."

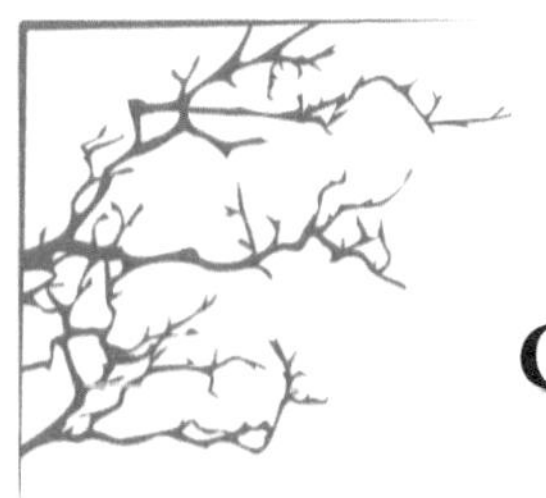

Chapter 16

"What the fuck? How do you know that?"

He merged right again, earning an extended honk for his effort. In seconds he was on the southbound ramp, merging at speed.

Lila was still all hunched over but now she was emitting a low grinding hum.

"Are you malfunctioning???" he shouted.

"It was like I heard him, and it felt like stabbing. Then I saw Bruce and they were in the Haight."

"Who's Bruce? Who did you hear?"

She sat up and ran her hands through her hair. Her knees came up to guard her chest.

"Emil. The one who turned me. I think I just accidentally read his mind."

"And he's in San Francisco?"

"Yeah, with one of his other vampires. Bruce."

"And that's who you're running away from?"

The truck dunked into a pothole. Cash swore.

"Why are they looking for you?"

Lila sighed again.

"It might be because I stole a bunch of money from their vault. But I think mostly because I left."

"What are they going to do if they catch you? Stake you in the heart?"

"If I'm lucky. Worst case scenario they force me to go back to Los Angeles with them."

Golden West Diner had not changed an iota since Lila was last here. Not surprisingly. It hadn't changed an iota since 1983. Everything in it was nicotine stained and the theme was a mix of Elvis and John Wayne memorabilia.

Cash had made her promise she wasn't hungry before they came in, for the safety of any humans present. She wasn't hungry, not enough to lose her mind and commit mass murder in a diner anyway.

"Do we really have to stop here? You just ate a whole deer like twelve hours ago."

"Twelve hours too long."

The singular server led them to a Formica booth table yellowed with age.

"Hardly anyone's even in here for me to ravage with my bloodlust," Lila said after the waitress had taken his order (chicken fried steak, collard greens, and a strawberry milkshake).

She leaned against the wall of the booth, drowning in Cash's Thrasher sweatshirt.. The hood hung halfway down her face.

"What's with everything being too bright?" Cash asked. "I didn't know you were allergic to electric lights too."

"I'm not. It's just unpleasant. Humans like everything so bright."

His shake came and he downed half of it in one long slurp. Most of the time in human form he looked like a regular guy, but his manner of eating was markedly lupine.

"So you can't eat human food anymore." She shook her head. On the way she had filled him in on her entanglement with and escape from Emil. How Emil had made her and Sasha fetch him victims, and how he was so much stronger he could force them to do anything.

How Emil had starved her, not letting her leave the mansion, until one night he brought a girl who couldn't have even been eighteen home. He'd drained the girl in front of Lila, stopping at the precipice of death.

"Drink from her, vegetarian. Feel her pulse slow in your mouth." He had drug Lila

across the room by the hair, shoving her face at the girl's throat.

"DRINK!" he had screamed. Bruce and the fourth of their unholy quartet, Samson, had surrounded the couch. Emil wouldn't let them feed until this little scene was over and they were hungry.

Lila had twisted away from Emil's grip, just as Samson lost control and attacked the girl. His plans thwarted, Emil backhanded Lila, breaking the orbit of her eye socket with his unbridled strength. When she came too she was alone on the floor just before dawn. She had crawled to the basement crypt and into her coffin. Left alone to heal, she resolved to escape.

When she finished, Cash had begun asking questions and the questions had not stopped.

"What about water? No? Just blood every couple of days?"

She nodded.

"That's the deal."

"So why do vampires kill so many people?"

"The more you drink the stronger you get. And if you drain someone completely you get, like, a power burst. You can go out in the sun, even. At least, Emil can. He's really old though and you get stronger with age."

He nodded.

"This Emil. He turned you."

"Yeah,"

The waitress, in her goldenrod uniform dress and uninterested expression, brought the food. Cash began bolting down the steak.

"No one's gonna take it from you, dude," Lila said dryly. Cash paused, fork halfway to his mouth, and then chewed the bite in his mouth with big exaggerated chews. Then he lifted his milkshake with his pinky up and sipped it daintily.

He set the glass down and patted his lips with his napkin.

"I didn't criticize your table manners when you were chugging type A positive in my bedroom, madam."

She rolled her eyes.

"So this guy Emil, he kills people and thus has the power pack or whatever?"

"Correct."

"Where would you get the people you brought him?"

"I usually went to bars. Samson would go to methadone clinics."

"How much blood would you need to be as strong as Emil?"

Lila shook her head.

"He's like two hundred years old. I'll never be as strong as him."

"Whoa, that's old. AND he can read your mind?"

"Sorta? I'm not really sure how it works but sometimes he would be able to see what I was thinking. And I guess sometimes I can see his thoughts."

Cash chewed silently. Lila jiggled her leg. Anxiety addled her. She'd mixed Cash, one of the few truly kind people she'd ever met, up with Emil, the worst being on the West Coast.

"Cash... you shouldn't help me."

"Why's that?"

"Well, first of all, because there's no good reason for you to help me to begin with. Also, if you help me Emil and his idiots will target you too."

"No GOOD reason? Are there any bad reasons?"

"Ugh, shut up."

"Does this steak even smell good to you?"

"It doesn't smell gross, if that's what you mean."

"No, like do you have any desire to eat it?"

"None whatsoever. No more than you would want to eat grass."

He tilted his head at her and the resemblance to a puppy made her nearly laugh out loud.

"Oh, like this is your food's food?"

She nodded and smiled, showing her fangs a little. Cash laughed.

He polished off his steak and wiped his mouth, then slapped the napkin down on the table.

"Ready, Killer?"

The house was cold and dark when they got home. Cash flipped on the heater and turned on a few lamps. Nice and cozy, much better.

"Lila, do you - Lila? Where are you?"

"You have to invite me in."

He spun around to see Lila waiting at the threshold, her legs poking out from beneath his hoodie. Lila Phillips is wearing my hoodie, he thought, and the realization short circuited him.

"Cash! Invite me the frick in!"

"Sorry! Come in! Please!"

She huffed and stepped inside.

"Wait, is the garlic thing true too?"

"If you put any human food on or in me I am definitely going to have a reaction," Lila answered evenly. She flopped down on the couch.

Cash got a beer and sat at the other end.

"Here are all the reasons you should not help me. Number one. Emil is stronger, richer, and probably smarter than either of us. He also has three other vampires and a human that will do pretty much whatever he says."

"Right. Army of dipshits."

"Second, no offense, but werewolves are not as strong as vampires. I've seen Emil toss a wolfman like an orca tosses a seal."

Cash raised a brow. Lila grimaced.

"There are werewolves in LA?"

"Yeah. Of course. Listen to me though."

"Okay."

"Last, Emil is eventually going to figure out where I am. He found me in Palmdale I think by following my scent. I didn't tell Emil much about my life but he's smart. Vampires aren't too good with the internet but they can be very persuasive in person. And when he finds me he is going to kill you both for helping me and for... for being a werewolf in the first place."

Cash bent down to untie his boots. He toed them off and put his feet on the coffee table. Lila was curled up in a little ball up against the other arm of the couch. He wished he could bring her something to eat or drink.

"Boy. That's sure a pickle. Do you almighty vampires have any weaknesses?"

"Sunlight. Even a vampire at, uh, max power can only be in the sun for a short time."

"How long?"

"Fifteen minutes or so, from what I've seen."

Cash nodded. He sipped his beer.

"What else?"

"Have to be invited in. Can't eat human food or drink. Our eyes are super sensitive to light. Ummmm stake through the heart will definitely kill us."

She watched him. He sipped his beer.

"So you said the garlic thing doesn't work. How do we make vampire repellent?"

There is one scent Emil can't stand, Lila thought.

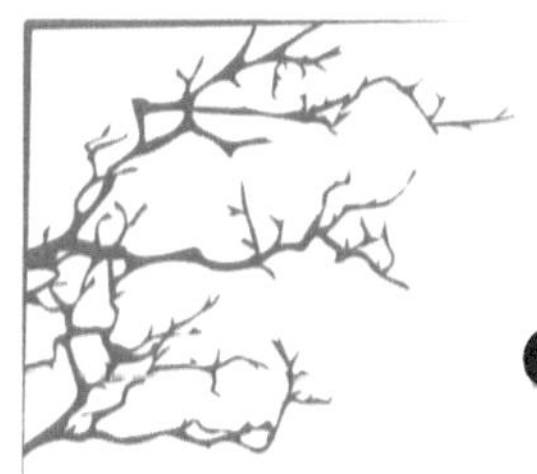

Chapter 17

"What does that look mean?" Cash asked, cocking his head sarcastically. .

"Uh, okay, so don't take this the wrong way."

"What."

"Emil hates the smell of dogs. It's disgusting to him."

Cash stared at her, his eyes hard.

"It's not what I think! It's just what he said all the time: werewolves and all canines are filthy. He hates your kind."

Cash blinked slowly and shook his head.

"So how do we use that to our advantage?"

"I'm not sure yet." She ran her fingers through her long hair. It was so glossy and thick. He watched it cascade over her shoulders.

"I think the scent of a dog helped me get away from him once before."

She told him about the friendly mutt that had shared his scent with her, down in the high desert.

"Huh. So my disgusting dog smell might actually protect you," Cash said drily.

"I didn't say it was disgusting," Lila defended herself.

"How long til you get hungry again?" Cash asked.

"Depends on how active I am. Maybe another night or two."

He nodded and drained his beer.

"You sure you don't want anything at all?" He went to the fridge.

"No. Unless you have a bloodsicle somewhere."

"Gross."

He settled back onto the couch. She tried to be patient. He was thinking, apparently.

"We can make the bedroom light proof. If you sleep in my bed you'll have a lot more of my scent on you. Hey, no funny business," he assured, raising his hands in front of him. "I'll mostly be awake when you're asleep and vice versa."

She frowned.

"You're in danger, Cash. Having me here endangers you. If he finds us he's just as likely to murder you as not."

"So you're saying I have a chance? Buck up, Killer. Let me be nice, since you think I'm such a big softy."

She sighed and shook her head.

"Your funeral. How do we do this alleged light proofing?"

Blankets, overlapping with each other, nailed to the wall and sealed with duct tape. That was how Cash planned to light proof his bedroom. One set of blankets on the window. One set outside the bedroom door, re-sealable with velcro.

"You just thought of that?"

"Yeah."

"Do you have all that stuff?"

"No, but I can go to the All Nite."

The All Nite was a massive, cheap department store on the eastern edge of Lawry. It was cavernous, lit with greenish fluorescent lights, and carried everything from camping supplies to baby shampoo to all weather tires. Lila had bought her first thong there in eighth grade. And her first condoms, in tenth grade.

"You stay here. It'll be safer. Cozy up in bed if you want to. No one will think twice if they see me out buying random shit at midnight. Everyone in town thinks I'm a tweaker anyway," he joked weakly.

"Are you sure? I - I have money," Lila offered. She reached under the thick hoodie she still wore, his hoodie, and into her fanny pack. She peeled a few hundred dollars off and handed them to him.

"Is that enough?"

"Jesus Christ, Killer." She winced. "No wonder these assholes want to find you. How much is that?"

She looked down at it.

"A hundred grand."

Cash whistled cartoonishly. He looked down at the hundreds.

"Is this gonna trace back to them somehow?"

"No. It's not from a bank. It's from people they've murdered and robbed over the years."

Cash frowned. He slipped the money into his wallet.

Lila took Cash's advice and got ready for bed. It wouldn't be dawn any time soon. But she was tired. And the more she slept, the less she had to feed. She took a quick shower, washing her hair and body all over with his fancy shampoo and soap and conditioner. Everything smelled good and came in a pretty bottle. She wondered if all werewolves had such a taste for luxury or just Cash. And if he liked expensive things so much why did he live in this little dump of a farmhouse?

She dried herself with Cash's characteristically fluffy, absorbent bath towels. One of the unsettling new truths about her body was that she was cold blooded - she took on the temperature of her environment. Since she had just been in a warm shower, her skin was warm, like a living being. When she slept in the mausoleum, she had woken up with skin as cold as marble.

Cash's room smelled half like his expensive shampoo and half like his dirty socks. She pulled what she hoped was a clean tee shirt off a pile of folded clothes on top of the chair. There was no way she was going to rifle through his dresser drawers and she couldn't find another pair of boxer briefs, so she hoped for the best.

The bed was imposing in its layers of comfiness. It was tall and fluffy, with a firm backbone. He had multiple types of pillows. His steel gray sheets were smooth and cool to the touch, and his duvet was heavy. She flipped the covers back and snuggled down.

The terror that spurred her, that had been on her since she moved into Emil's mansion, was muted in here. She knew Emil and Sasha and the others were still out there, looking for revenge. She couldn't let this... this comfort, or familiarity, whatever it was that she felt near Cash, she couldn't let it numb her to the reality that she was in danger. If she did it wouldn't just be her that paid.

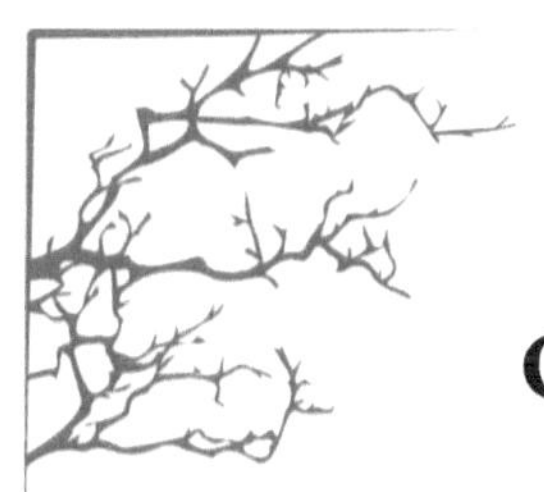

Chapter 18

The All Nite stood glowing stark and alone among the empty lots of southeastern Lawry. Cash parked under a broken parking lot light and grabbed a stray cart.

The place was busy this Saturday night. Even though he wasn't doing a single thing illegal, he didn't want to answer any questions. With any luck no one he knew would be here.

First up he grabbed a bottle of Laphroiag and a pack of frozen T-bones. The necessities. Next he headed down the camping aisle. Wooden tent stakes, they had to be here somewhere.

Moving blankets. Duct tape. Velcro. Fabric glue. He headed to the women's apparel area. He was one hundred percent sure Lila would never willingly wear All Nite Couture but she could at least have some stuff of her own instead of his clothes. A 6 pack of undies in what he hoped was her size, a couple of pairs of leggings, and some cotton tank tops. He stared at the rack of bras, wondering if he could possibly guess which would fit.

"Cash, oh my god!"

He looked behind him. A blonde woman in workout clothes.

"It's me! Dana. You, um, wired my dad's store?" She faltered, thrown off by his blank expression. She glanced down at his cart and her eyes went wide before she recovered.

"Oh! Right. Hey. Sorry. How are you?"

He didn't bother to explain the contents of his cart. She'd just have to believe he was a serial killer.

"Good! The store's doing really well, and, oh, are you in a hurry? I'm sorry."

"What? Oh, good god, sorry, I am actually kind of." He forced his foot to stop tapping.

"Oh, cool, okay. Well, text me some time, or whatever," she said, looking mildly alarmed.

"Yeah, totally, yes," he said. He was being so rude. Plus now the owner's daughter thought he was a murderer. They would never hire him again. Shit.

Dana walked off, shaking her head slightly. Cash grabbed a couple of bras without looking and headed for the cereal aisle.

Cargo stowed, he pulled out his phone. He wanted to check in with his family, see if they knew anything about vampires. Not his mother though. She would tell her sister, and then the whole family would know and it would be a whole thing. No. He would call his cousin Carter.

"Baby boy," Carter growled into the phone.

"Hey dickhead," Cash purred back.

"Where've you been?" Carter's voice was so deep it was hard to understand sometimes.

"Not you, too, man. I couldn't get time off for the reunion, okay? I'm only a journeyman."

"Fuckin sensitive aren't you?"

"Yeah yeah. Anyway, are you busy?"

Cash heard Carter take a drag off what he assumed was a joint.

"Not at all. What's up?"

"You ever met a vampire?"

He could hear Carter sit up and take notice over the phone.

"No, thank fuck, I've never met a vampire. Why do you ask?"

"I have one at my house currently."

"What, like, locked in a box?"

"I imagine she's in the bathroom taking a shower, actually."

"Cash tell me you're not banging a vampire."

"Would that be bad?"

Carter groaned.

"All I know is every wolf I've ever talked to avoids vampires like tweakers avoid the dentist. They're dangerous. And they have like, mind control powers."

"Okay now you just sound stupid," Cash scoffed.

"For real. Stay away from them. Stake the one you've got in the heart and burn the body."

"I'll take that under advisement."

"The false hope of the man horny for vampire ass. Good luck, dummy."

Cash started the truck, shaking his head.

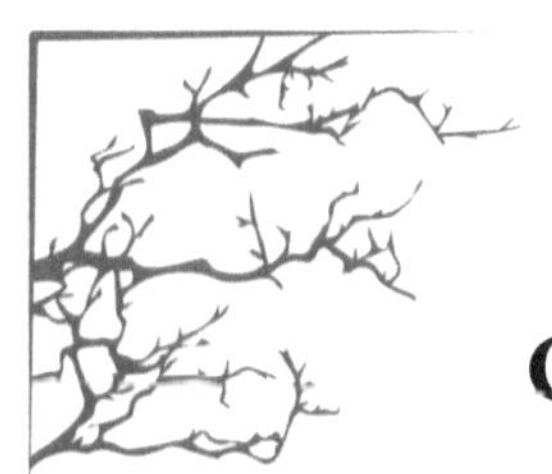

Chapter 19

His cousins loved to treat him like he was a dumb little kid. His whole family. Just because he'd been a late bloomer. When he finally turned, he flipped out to his mom the next day.

"How could you not tell me? What if it happened when I was driving? Or... or at school?"

"Honey," his mom had soothed with her yoga voice. "I thought I had time. We all thought it wouldn't be until your Saturn Return."

Apparently he was a genetic sport. His shifts had started at eighteen, at his nodal return. Most weres started shifting at either their Jupiter or Saturn returns. Age twelve or twenty eight. Another aspect of lycanism no one could explain to him.

"I'm sorry, baby boy. You turned out to be a beautiful wolf."

He carried a load of blankets inside through the carport door.

"Hey Lila," he said," then stopped short at his bedroom door. She was all curled up, asleep, in his bed. She looked delicate, her long dark hair spread over his pillow. Carter's words came back to him. Dangerous. Maybe most vampires were but it was hard to picture that little thing hurting him, with his big claws and teeth. She was just scared and alone. His heart tugged at him. Back in school there had been rumors about her home life, and none of them had been pleasant. She had no one.

He had planned to get her to help him bring all the stuff in but he couldn't bring himself to wake her. Instead he set the bag of clothes on top of his dresser and closed the door behind him.

Lila opened her eyes. The bedroom was pitch dark. She sighed in the sheer luxury of it - a whole bedroom that was as dark as Emil's crypt. And the comforting illusion of safety.

Cash was next to her, on top of the covers facing away, breathing the long even cadence of someone deeply asleep. His hair was its normal mass of brown corkscrews threaded with gold. His broad shoulders moved with his breaths.

Emil's hatred of shifters came to mind. He said they were filthy, smelly, and primitive, but Cash was none of those things. He was smart and sweet, and smelled amazing.

A longing to touch him overcame her. To touch him, and to drink from him. She could feel how alive he was, more full of life force than a human, practically glowing with it. His blood would be so hot and plentiful. It would fill her up so easily.

She couldn't though. It might ruin her existing abilities. It might curse her with opposing abilities - weakest and strongest at the full moon. For all she knew werewolf blood might light her fangs on fire. Sasha had implied that it was basically poison to a vampire.

Cash rolled over. She waited to see if he would wake up but he didn't. His dark lashes stayed still on his strong cheeks. He was so... pretty. Deep brown freckles sparsely dusted his wide nose and cheeks, and his lips looked like they'd been carved from rose quartz and polished to a perfect sheen.

She remembered his arm clotheslining her in the forest. His strong, thick arm, literally sweeping her off her feet. Then he'd pinned her down, his hot thighs on either side of her. His throat mere inches from her teeth.

Lila shuddered at the remembered bloodlust. Here he was in front of her, so helpless, his neck totally unprotected. He would never be able to fight her off, not if she surprised him... She shook her head. She wouldn't do that to him. He deserved to be safe from her, not to be her food.

Through force of will she rose from the comfort of the bed and debated digging through one of the piles of clothes for some sort of bottoms. Then she saw the All Nite bag and looked inside.

Chapter 20

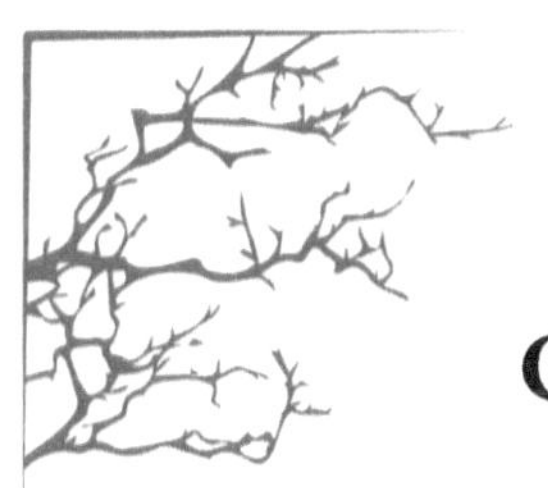

Leggings. A pack of panties, not the thongs she normally wore but cotton briefs. A random assortment of bralettes. All black.

He had gotten her clothes. Most of them wouldn't fit, but he had tried - he even made sure to get only black stuff.

Lila glanced behind her, confirming that he was still fast asleep. She pulled Cash's tee shirt over her head and slid into some of the leggings. To her surprise they fit fine, and were so soft. Lovely. The panties she could wear to sleep in but they wouldn't work under the leggings. Of the bralettes only one, a low impact sports bra, was the right size. She dragged it over her head and under her boobs, then put the tee shirt back on.

Being helped like this, especially without having asked, felt strange. She would find a way to repay him since she could plainly see the bills she had given him sticking out of his wallet next to the All Nite bag.

She checked the clock radio next to Cash's side of the bed. Eight PM. Wow, she had slept almost twenty four hours. This time of year it would definitely be night time out, but she was a little scared anyway.

Gingerly, both in fear of the sun and to keep from waking Cash, she snuck out of the bedroom and closed the door behind her. To her surprise, there was a wall of blankets affixed to the wall with velcro. He had done all the light proofing himself, while she slept. She blinked. Slowly, desperate not to make a sound, she undid the velcro and slipped through, only to find a second blanket.

Free from the noisy velcro prison, she padded out to the common area of the little house.

The kitchen island was piled with torn open packaging, All Nite bags, and empty duct tape roles. She began to tidy up.

Someone knocked on the door. Lila froze. They knocked again, louder.

"Cash! I know you're home. Wake up!" A female voice yelled from the front stoop.

Lila crept close to the door. She peeked through the peephole.

A woman a head shorter than Lila, with black hair and green bangs, stood on the stoop. Lila didn't know what to do. This lady could be anyone. This could be Cash's fucking girlfriend, for all Lila knew. In fact it probably was Cash's girlfriend and here Lila was letting herself think about... whatever she was thinking about. Wrath filling her, Lila momentarily forgot she was wearing Cash's tee shirt, and flung the door open.

"Hi," said the woman on the stoop. Her fist was in the air about to pound on the door again. She had long, stabby black nails and a rosary tattoo on the back of her hand. "Is Cash here?"

"Who are you?"

"Who exactly the fuck are you?" she snapped. "Cash! Where have you been dude?"

"Tell me who you are and what you want or I'm putting you back in your car," Lila said, crossing her arms over her chest.

"Are you, like, his bodyguard?"

Lila stared at her. She wasn't even doing anything vampiric, just her normal intensely rude expression. The tiny one rolled her eyes and relented.

"I'm Carolina. Cash was supposed to get lunch with me today but he hasn't been answering his phone so I got worried."

Lila wrinkled her nose. If this was Cash's girlfriend, she was being very casual about another woman being in her man's house in his clothes.

"Okay, come in I guess," Lila said. She stepped aside and Carolina came in.

"I like your outfit," Lila said, plopping on the couch.

"Really? Thanks. It's all thrifted pretty much. Except my creepers." She stuck her foot out to show Lila her shoes, which had bat wings.

"Those are pretty cute," Lila chuckled. She stretched her arms above her head. Carolina came around to the couch and sat down, arranging her legs under her.

"Where did you get your fangs done?" Carolina asked. "They look hella cool."

"What?" Lila tongued her fangs, startled. She had fucking forgotten about her fangs, and made no attempt to hide them.

"They look sick. Did you get them done at like a dentist? I heard in TJ you can get them done pretty cheap."

"TJ?"

"Hey Caro," Cash rumbled behind them. "Nice of you to stop by."

"Dude! You scared me."

Lila watched Carolina not stare at Cash's bare body. Stare at Cash's body was all Lila wanted to do.

Snap out of it dummy, she chastised herself.

"Hey we were supposed to get lunch today and you didn't even text me. I was worried."

"Aw, shit. I'm sorry. My sleep's been all out of whack. I slept all day," Cash said remorsefully. He sat between the two of them, in the corner of the sectional. Lila saw his gaze linger on her leggings, an expression like contentment on his face.

"Are you sick?" Carolina asked. Her eyes flicked to Lila and back. Cash gazed at Carolina for an extra second. Lila liked that, how Cash would take a second before answering sometimes. Like he thought things through.

"I'm not sick. This is Lila by the way. She went to high school with us. She's back in town."

Carolina looked at Lila, then at Cash, then Lila again.

"Ooookay."

"Lila, this is Carolina, my best friend."

"Pleased to meet you," Lila said.

"So why did you sleep all day?"

"I had a long night. Plus I switched." Cash got back up from the couch and went to the kitchen.

How many people know he's a werewolf? Lila wondered.

"Awww, he's all tuckered out," Carolina said in a sarcastically sweet singsong. Lila barely heard her. She was watching the dark line of Cash's treasure trail bend and twist as he moved around the kitchen, pulling out leftover pizza and eating it while Carolina told him about the guest on her radio show that morning. The sight was making her tongue throb with thirst. His abs were so shredded she could see the veins over his Adonis belt. Even through the hair.

Wait a sec. Radio show? That's pretty cool.

"Do you think you could sell me some of your clothes?" Lila blurted.

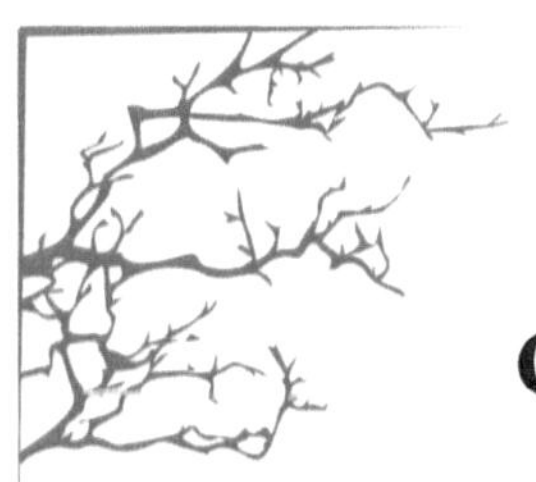

Chapter 21

arolina paused for a second, head cocked.

"Girl... we're not the same size," Carolina said looking back and forth between them.

Carolina was about six inches shorter than her and their proportions were nearly opposite. Lila cackled. It sounded like it was coming through an ancient radio.

"Fuck," she wheezed. Carolina and Cash stared at her. She hacked wetly. Finally she recovered and brushed her hair back behind her shoulders. "Is that shitty bar on Monterey still there?"

"What, Acorn Hutch?"

"Yeah. Can we go there?"

"It's Sunday night. It's gonna be so dead in there," Cash said.

"Even better.

Carolina and Cash looked at each other. Cash shrugged. Carolina nodded.

"Great. Can I borrow some clothes at least? It's okay if it's short."

An hour later Cash was driving Lila and Carolina to the Acorn Hutch, the absolute worst bar in town. Well, a little outside of town.

It was weirdly lit and always had the most random sports blaring from one tv, like falconry and professional lacrosse. It attracted the most annoying people from miles around. Cash knew Lila needed to feed but this was a lot to ask.

Plus, they might run into someone who knew her from high school. None of Cash's friends hung out at the Acorn but Lila had been part of a different (albeit overlapping) circle back then. Her weird older boyfriends, who knew what they were doing nowadays. Maybe they were the type of drink spikers who hung out at this place.

The more people knew she was here the more likely it would somehow get to Emil. Cash racked his brain for anyone in Lawry who might have a connection to LA vampires.

He pulled the truck into the parking lot with its one orangey light.

"Lila, are you sure this is a good idea?"

She checked her face in the visor mirror.

"No. Are you sure it's a bad idea?"

He frowned.

"What if you know someone in there?"

"No one's going to know it's me," Lila stated confidently. She opened the passenger door and hopped out.

Carolina had lent her a black satin dress. It was a knee length pencil silhouette on Caro, but on Lila it was short and skimpy as hell. She had curled her long dark hair so it cascaded down her back, and her eyes were framed by smokey black makeup.

The wolf in Cash was going nuts. Her scent was so LOUD with all her skin uncovered like that, her scent that had invaded his house and his nose, the scent of dead blood and lilies. The man in him, the human man, was also not immune to her.

Down, boy, he told himself. He and Carolina got out of the truck and followed Lila into the bar.

This place was the spiritual opposite of El Greco. It was ugly and uncool from its gray carpet to the beer company flags and neons decorating the walls. Four separate televisions, all with volume on, displayed sports and commercials. The jukebox, which was connected to the internet, played croony adult contemporary country. The pleather bar stools were all cracked. Cash hated every inch of the Acorn Hut.

When the trio walked in, the room paused for a moment to look at them, then went back to its noisy brightly lit activities. Two shiny haired twenty something guys in golf shirts played pool. Another few golf beshirted men sat at the bar. A clutch of them were gathered around one particular television, watching a sport with which Cash was unfamiliar. Carolina and Lila were the only women in the place.

Lila slid up to the bar. Sideways glances from across the room at her round ass in the tight skirt. Cash frowned.

He and Carolina joined Lila at the bar. The bartender, a bored twenty one year old enby, came over and looked at them expectantly.

"A soda water with lime and mint for me please. And whatever my friends want," Lila's voice dripped off her pointed tongue, honeyed and lilting. Her frame blurred slightly, like a mirage. A few of the sidelong glances gave way to head-turned stares. Cash looked around the bar, confused. That hazy shimmer was everywhere, on the edges of his vision.

"Well, what the frick do you want?" the barkeep asked. Cash shook his head and looked at them. They shook their hand impatiently at him.

"Uh, Laphroaig neat," he said. His lunar tendencies were stirring and he needed a strong, mean drink to distract his senses.

"IPA please," Carolina said.

Lila leaned against a stool. Her pupils were pinholed like a cat about to pounce.

"What are you doing?" Cash murmured. It smelled like pheromones and protein, lilies and mildew.

"I guess you would call it," Lila purred, in her syrupy voice, "softening the room."

"Can you tone it down," he rasped. Her eyes shot up to his. They flashed at her, reflected gold like a harvest moon. His lip curled like he was holding in a snarl. "Everyone in here wants to fuck your brains out. No skips."

"No skips?"

His eyes bored into hers.

"No skips."

She smirked, her fangs glistening. Her gaze slid away from him and landed on a mark across the room. Cash searched the mirror behind the bar for her target.

He was spike haired, blonde, sunglasses in his collar as he bent to make a pool shot. His massive traps and lats under his silky gray golf shirt made it clear he spent all his time away from the office at the gym. Cash didn't recognize him. This bar was halfway between Lawry and San Simon. People who lived on the southern edge of San Simon liked to think they were a lot better than the hicks in Lawry, even though these days as many people in Lawry worked and went to school in San Simon as didn't. These guys, and guys they were, must live in San Simon. If they weren't being hypnotized they would probably resent having a bunch of South County trash in "their" bar.

Lila smiled slowly. Cash watched as Blondie tipped his head at his fellows, and made a beeline for the bar. Cash stayed put, facing the bar, watching in the mirror. Carolina went over to the jukebox.

"Can I buy you a drink?" Blondie asked, over-confident in his vascular forearms.

"Yeah, you wanna do a shot?" Lila suggested. In the mirror, the back of her head tilted. He imagined her looking up at Blondie through her thick, dark lashes.

The bartender brought two little glasses of something. Cash forced himself to pretend he wasn't concerned with how this guy was touching Lila's arm, how she was laughing at his stupid comments.

He sipped his Laphroaig. The smokiness filled his mouth and nose, obliterating every other scent. The hackles of his inner wolf went back down.

Next he knew Lila and Blondie were getting up to go outside for "a cigarette." As Lila stepped out the door the strange shimmer receded from the room, sliding out the door with her. He took a deep breath and finished his whiskey.

Carolina came back over and sat on the stool next to him.

"You still have it so bad for her, don't you?"

"Ugh."

"Is she just gonna go fuck that guy? That has to bug you. Not trying to stir shit up or whatever but that's kinda sus."

"She's not here to fuck anyone," Cash gritted out. The idea of that oaf touching Lila under her clothes was making his blood boil.

"If you say so."

Carolina looked extremely dubious. Cash wanted to explain that Lila was just going to suck that guy's blood, nothing fishy, but it didn't seem like the right time to introduce vampires into her worldview.

"For an internet jukebox there's nothing good on there," Caro complained.

"I know right?" the bartender agreed, rolling their eyes. "I hear Push You at least twice a night."

Cash tried to focus on their banter but his senses were all on high alert, hearing every sound in the room. He stared into his whisky glass.

"Another for you, baby?"

Carolina had softened up the bartender enough that their sarcastic, bored visage had dropped. She was good at that.

"Yeah, another Scotch please."

"So polite."

After what felt to Cash like three quarters of an hour, Lila came back. She slid liquidly onto the stool to his right. He allowed himself to glance down at her.

She was glowing. Her skin had taken on a blush, a sheen. Her hair looked bouncier, and her eyes were wet and black. She grinned at him. Her fangs were still pinkish and she ran her tongue over them

"Feel better?"

She nodded, satisfied.

"Can we go now?"

She nodded and leaned her shoulder against him for the briefest second, like a cat rubbing its scent on his leg. He felt a prickle up the back of his neck at her touch.

Cash looked over his shoulder, seeking out Blondie. There he was, back at the pool table, a dopey smile spread across his face. Only a little paler for it, and with two little bite marks peeking out from his shirt collar. A bolt of jealousy shot through Cash. He frowned and followed Lila.

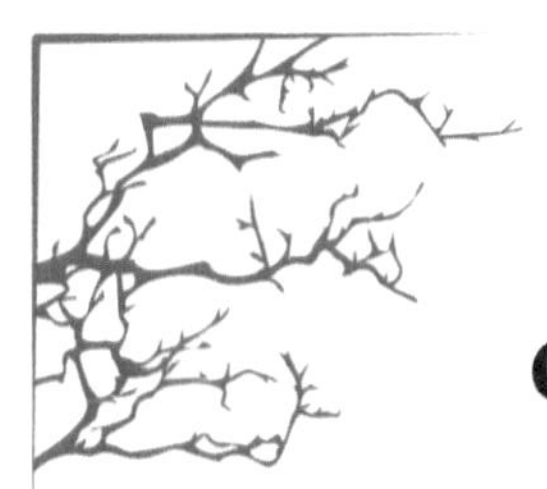

Chapter 22

She led the three of them back out to his truck. The energy she had gained from feeding crackled off her, an arcing transformer. She could have thrown a car over a building. Cash opened the passenger door. Carolina hopped in, sliding into the middle seat without so much as a glance at Lila. Lila was too blood drunk to notice but Cash did.

"Can you just take me back to my car?" Carolina said flatly.

They drove in silence back to Cash's remote farmhouse.

"Caro - " Cash started, but she jumped out and got in her Prius with a tossed- out goodbye.

"What's the matter?" Lila asked. Even with her veins singing like this she could see that Cash was disgruntled.

"Caro just fuckin bounced."

Lila hummed noncommittally.

"She never does that. I wonder what her problem is."

"Feel better?" Cash asked, cracking open a beer. He leaned on the kitchen counter and followed Lila with his eyes. Her body moved different, smooth and silky like a dancer, and she still had that glowy sheen. She glided through the room and folded herself onto the sofa. He wasn't worried about Carolina anymore. It took all his focus to keep from transforming, to keep from leaping over the back of the couch and pinning Lila to the cushions.

He went to the record player and put on some Bay Area sludge metal. Lila got up on her knees, still in her skintight satin dress, and leaned her forearms on the back of the couch. She watched him open another beer.

"You've been keeping me up awfully late, Ms Phillips."

"Would you like to go to bed, Mr Mosely?"

He shut his eyes. His fangs were stretching, getting sharper. He shook his head, and opened his eyes. Lila was staring at him, biting her lip, her eyes heavy and dark.

His skin rippled, and thick fur sprouted from his neck, his chest, the backs of his hands. Back arched, he threw his jacket off just as his muscles bulged and his body ripped open his tee shirt. Claws tore his fingertips open and his ears stretched to thickly furred points. His face rearranged into a short snout, tipped with a wet black nose. Fangs sprang from his gums. He shook all over and his transformation was complete. He had taken on his half-wolf form, in which he could walk upright and talk.

"Fuck," Lila gasped.

Cash turned his monstrous head towards her and snorted, then bolted out the door to the back patio. Seconds later she heard him howl, lonely and long.

"That was so fucking sexy," she sighed to no one. She stared after him, wondering if he would be back any time soon. Meanwhile the night fog was flowing in.

Lila got up and slid the back door shut, taking care to leave it unlocked.

When Cash got home, panting and steaming in the foggy cold, it was early Monday morning. He texted Nilo that he wouldn't be in until after lunch.

Lila must be asleep, he figured. Rather than disturb her twice, he got straight in the shower to get the animal gore and mud off. He wanted to give himself a moment to truly let the wild bed back down before he was in the same room with her, anyway.

Muscles aching and feet sore, he washed his hair with his rich shampoo and conditioner. He let the steam rise around him as he painstakingly detangled his mane while the conditioner soaked in.

His father's mom had taught him a lot about his hair before she passed. His father, a Marine, had been killed in action when Cash was six. His white mom had no idea how to take care of hair like his, so every weekend at Grandma's, she would teach him.

Then when Cash was fourteen, his Grandma passed away too.

Not that being at Mom's full time was so bad. His mother had been a waitress, working at the casino south of town all weekend. Her sister, Carter's mom, would come live with them for a few months at a time. Or she'd leave the kids, Carter and Orion, while she went on tour. Both women were rock n roll hippies, restless hearts. There was always family in and out, and never a dull moment.

He rinsed and shut the water off.

Now Carter was in San Francisco, Orion was in Las Balenas, and his mom and aunt had retired to the desert with some other werewolves of their generation. When Cash thought about it all, a bone-deep lonesomeness took him. He missed being part of a big bunch of people who all knew about this.

He toweled off, patting his hair dry gently before running product through it. It had taken him dozens of tries to find hair stuff that smelled good to his wolf nose.

Next came cocoa butter.

Clean and moisturized, Cash wrapped his towel around his waist and carefully went through the two layers of curtains.

It took even his sharp eyes a moment to adjust to the absolute darkness inside, punctuated by the red numbers of his clock radio. When he did, he saw Lila's ghostly gray form sitting up in his bed. She had one one of his white undershirts. His breath shuddered out.

"Are you awake?" he murmured.

"I couldn't sleep," she said.

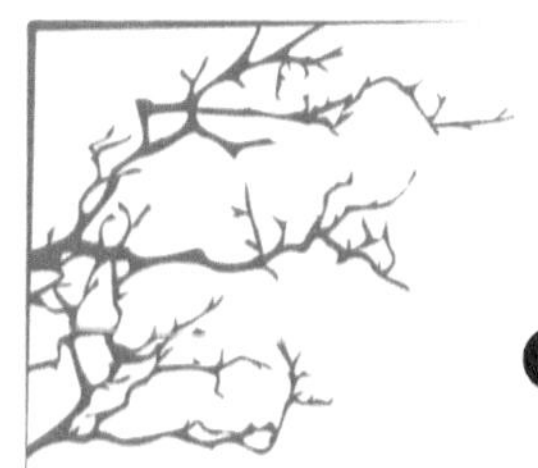

Chapter 23

Her voice had lost that extra slip it had had at the bar.

"I need to, uh, I'm gonna get dressed," he muttered.

He turned his back to her and got underwear out of his dresser. He wiggled into it without dropping his towel. Lila may have seen him transform into a beast from fable last night, but he felt weird about her seeing him naked.

"Is it okay if I lie down?" he asked. "Need to sleep a couple hours."

"Of course. It's your bed," she demurred.

He got in. She was on top of the comforter so he got underneath.

"Will you still get my scent on you even if I just took a shower?" he said.

"I dunno. You smell pretty good, not wolfy at all," she answered, a touch of dreaminess in her voice that made him want to lean closer. He swallowed.

"What did you do at the bar? I mean... what was that?"

"I learned it from Sasha. Emil's girlfriend."

"Was it like mass hypnosis?"

She looked down at her hands.

"It was only supposed to hit one person but I can't really control it that well. I was focusing too much on not doing you and Carolina."

"Mighty big of you."

"I try."

"How do you do it?" He rolled onto his side facing her, and propped his head up on his hand.

"It's actually kinda silly. You know when you were a little kid and you would pretend you were like, shooting lasers out of your eyes?"

Cash chuckled.

"Yeah."

"That's kind of how it is. I like, think really hard about sending... mind control... rays."

Cash guffawed.

"Shut up, oh my god. It's so embarrassing."

"Okay so you shoot the rays. What does that feel like?"

"Like flexing a muscle inside my brain. Or, like pushing really hard against something inside my skull."

Cash nodded.

"So what does that feel like for the poor sucker you do it to?"

"It feels amazing. It feels like the sun picked just you to shine on. And whatever I ask for, you feel like it's a favor to you to get to do it. And I can sort of read your mind, just quick flashes."

He blew air through his lips. He was so fucked. He felt that way looking at her and she'd never even glamored him.

Lila's corpse-pale face approximated an embarrassed blush.

"Don't look at me like that. I know it's horrible."

"It's taking advantage, isn't it? Like not very consensual. "

Lila looked down. She let out a shuddering breath.

"I thought it would be okay because I saw that guy had roofies in his pocket."

"No fucking way!" Cash scooted up towards her. "That's what you read in his mind?"

"Yeah, basically. I just... I really needed to feed." She looked down at her balled up hands again. "And I figured it would be better to find some asshole, you know? I guess I didn't want to ask Spencer again."

Cash put his hand over hers, and gave her a quick squeeze.

"I'm not judging you. You have to eat."

She shook her head. Her black brows were knit together. She put the fist that Cash wasn't squeezing up to her lips, to keep herself from crying.

"I didn't want to be like this. I never asked for it."

Cash let his thumb rub hers, lightly, just letting her know he was still here. He wanted to hold her and tell her it was all gonna be okay, he wanted that so bad.

"Why are you helping me? Why are you being nice to me?" she asked suddenly. She picked up the hand Cash had been holding and wiped her eyes roughly.

Fuck. Cash thought. *That was too much. I went too far.*

"Um, I... I guess I just-" He fumbled. Should he come out and say it, that he'd had a crush on her since before she had gotten his biggest bully, Liam, to leave him alone? Should he say the scent of her was driving him mad with animal lust and all he wanted to do was take care of her?

"Nevermind, that's such a rude question. I'm sorry. I have no manners," she chastised herself, smiling weakly. "Thank you for allowing me to stay here, and keeping me safe."

Lila met his eyes and then shut hers and rolled over on her side, away from him. Cash rolled on his back and tried to let sleep take him.

Even after Cash left for work, Lila couldn't sleep. She was full of energy from just having fed. And all of that energy was devoted to anxiety.

Emil could be in Lawry now, just waiting, watching. He could have posted Samson or Cody outside the house, waiting to ambush her. Emil couldn't come inside here, not unless Cash invited him, but Cody could.

She burrowed deeper into the covers. Cash's wolfy scent wafted around her. God, he smelled so good. She rolled over and rubbed her face in the pillows.

I'm being totally weird, she thought. *Then again this whole situation is incredibly weird.*

Why was Cash helping her? And why did he have to go to work today? It was not helping her anxiety that he was out there, where Emil could find him. Emil had no way of knowing Cash even existed - Lila had never mentioned him - but Emil was incredibly talented, and incredibly persistent. All that was saving her right now was that she had told him she was from San Francisco, because she was ashamed of Lawry.

She thought of Emil's smarmy pinkish face, all angles, all sarcastically arched eyebrows. His silvery blonde hair like it had been hit with a weedwacker. He was always cutting it himself out of boredom.

Everything he did was out of boredom, or for power. Often both. And Sasha, everything she did was to maintain her proximity to Emil. By the end, Lila had wondered why Sasha was so beholden to Emil. She was nearly as powerful a vampire as him, and could easily have found her own retinue of minions in some other city. Instead she chose to be a glorified servant to the unpredictable, sadistic Emil.

Maybe she's afraid he'll hunt her down, she thought.

Lila sat up in bed. If she was going to rely so thoroughly on Cash for her safety she should make herself useful. She made the bed, navigating flawlessly in the pitch black of the room. Next, she put all his clothes back in the closet, from the first night when he had thrown them all over the place to make a spot for her.

After hanging up the clothes she began neatly organizing the floor of the closet. She hoped it wasn't intrusive to do this. He might freak out and get mad or something. But it felt worse to just sit in here and do nothing with him literally risking his life for her **for no reason**.

Fueled by racing thoughts, Lila proceeded in her organizational fury.

Cash checked his phone on his fifteen. He had texted Carolina on his way to work to see if she wanted to get dinner. But she still hadn't answered. He chewed his lip. Spencer on the other hand had texted him four times.

Bro what's going on w Lila

Hey dude wyd

(a meme about Baja Blast)

Oh I forgot you're at work lol

Cash smiled. He tucked his phone away and went back to work.

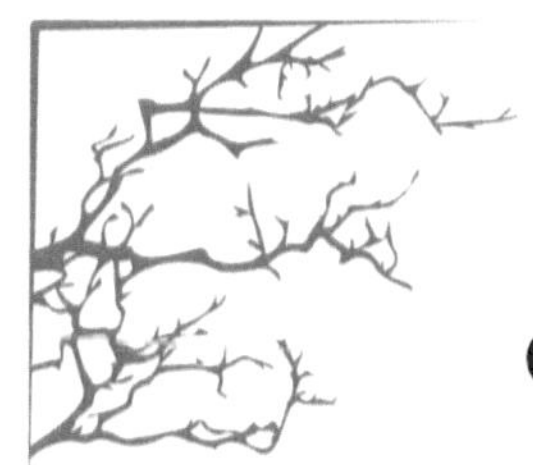

Chapter 24

By the time he was getting in his truck, Cash's stomach was already growling. He had eaten a steak at Golden West on the way into work, but that was long gone. Transforming last night had burned through a lot of reserves.

He pulled his headband off and threw the truck in reverse.

It was getting hard to control himself around Lila. This was bad. Whatever was going to happen with Emil better happen soon or he was going to say something truly nuts, and scare her off even worse than he already probably had.

At this point, she was most likely thinking he was helping because he wanted to fuck her. He needed to be a perfect gentleman and make it clear he respected her boundaries.

Carolina still hadn't texted him back. His brows knit together.

He punched the call button.

"Ugh, you woke me up," she answered on the fourth ring.

"You wanna get dinner? I'm on my way back from work. I could pick you up."

Scrabbling noises. The sound of her glugging water.

"You're not having dinner with Lila?"

Cash frowned. How to explain that Lila had already eaten.

"No. Definitely not."

"Oh."

"So, should I pick you up?"

"No. I need to get some more sleep. I don't usually stay up so late on Sundays because of the show."

"Oh. Right. See you -"

"See you," she hung up.

Cash irritably smacked the turn signal on to change lanes.

Driving faster than was strictly prudent, Cash arrived home just as the sun was setting. Today the sunset had taken on an autumnal crispness, a forewarning of the chill to come.

Cash whipped open the fridge and grabbed a rotisserie chicken half. He ripped off a wing and degloved it in a few seconds. From the window over the kitchen sink, he could see the sun's last few rays sinking into a dip in the hills.

He drank a big glass of water and cracked open a beer with the churchkey on his wallet chain. After a few sips enjoyed leaning on the counter, he headed towards his bedroom.

He unstuck the first curtain and re-stuck it, then the second. He opened the door but it was still pitch black inside.

"Lila?" he muttered. His cousin's words came back to him and the hair on his neck stood up. He was in a pitch black room with a vampire who wasn't answering.

Cash whipped his hand out to turn on the light, his body moving automatically into a defensive posture.

Lila had her back to him, and his big can headphones on. When the light came on she jumped a mile, a handful of Allen wrenches scattering all over his desk. She tore the cans off and spun around to look at him. The sound of double time kick drums leaked from the headphones.

"Motherfucker you scared me," she gasped.

"What are you listening to?" Cash asked. He tried not to lick his lips. Lila had on those leggings he'd picked up for her, and one of his undershirts that was doing nothing to hide the outlines of her curves.

"What???? Oh. Um, Cradle of Filth?" She picked up the record sleeve to show him.

"You like that???"

"Yeah, it's cool."

Cash looked around.

"You cleaned my room," he commented, at a loss. Surfaces were cleaned and tidied that he had forgotten even existed.

"Yeah, is that okay? I hope that's not like presumptuous or something." She picked at her nails.

"Not at all. I really appreciate it. Um, I'm super hungry. Do you want to ride with me to Taco Bell? I mean, if you're, like, bored of being in here."

She nodded.

"Super bored to be honest. Can I borrow your hoodie again?"

"I need to get gas first," Cash said as they barrelled down the road into town. Lila rolled

her window down. After being indoors for so long the air was refreshing.

Cash slowed down and turned into the Pegasus on the corner of First. He got out to pay Cash, and to his surprise Lila hopped out too.

"I, um, I dunno, I feel safer with you," she mumbled. His hoodie hung down past her butt, a lump at her hips where her ubiquitous fanny pack sat, and it made her look so fragile. He followed her into the quick mart.

Lila went to look at the magazines and Cash grabbed a six pack. Might as well since they were here. They met at the checkout.

"You two, huh?"

Lila looked up sharply.

"Liam. Wow," she said, dry as a bone.

"What's up, Cash," Liam said snidely, looking him up and down. Liam had a way of making your own name sound like the worst insult.

Cash adjusted himself pointedly, while making intense eye contact with Liam. He said nothing.

"That's twenty eight bucks plus forty for the gas," Liam muttered, looking down. He leered at Lila, until Cash coughed in a way that sounded exactly like a growl. He dropped his chin, gazing down at Liam until Liam handed him back his change.

Lila raised her eyebrow at him while they walked back to the truck.

"Big alpha wolf, huh?"

Cash looked at her in surprise, then shook his head.

"More like a lone wolf," Cash grunted, sticking the gas nozzle in.

He hopped in and started her up.

"You should let me eat Liam," Lila said.

"Now, now, Killer, no need to defend my honor."

"No seriously. He deserves it for so many reasons, not least of which is that horrible little goatee."

Cash pulled out of the gas station. He gunned it a little, just to be a prick to Liam.

"What are you, a vigilante? Vigilante vampire?"

"Yeah. Vampire crimefighter. Come on, you can be the bad cop," Lila teased, pushing his shoulder lightly.

Her touch raised his blood pressure. He pushed his hair back.

"Time to live mas."

They pulled into the line for the Taco Bell drive through. The one across town, which they both agreed offered the superior tortilla creations. The line of cars ahead of them proved it was where the people of Lawry went.

"What're you going to get?" Lila asked from under the oversized hood of his black Slayer sweatshirt. She had taken it off the couch where he'd left it when he'd left it when he got home. It was probably still a little warm when she put it on. He tried to remember that she was enveloping herself in his *scent*, not possessively ornamenting herself.

"Honestly I love a Chalupa."

"Interesting. You're a texture guy?"

"Yeah, I guess so. I mean that's what you're really picking at the Bell, right? Everything has the same flavor and different textures."

"Wow. A philosopher. I had no idea."

He shifted gears and pulled forward with the line.

"*This is Carolina Skeletina and you're listening to KRKC. Next up, Power Trip with 'Hornet's Nest.'*"

"Whoa," Lila said, sitting up. "That is so random, that's the band I was listening to earlier."

"Yeah. They're one of her favorites," Cash confirmed.

"Carolina's so cool," Lila said.

The line moved again.

"Do you remember her from high school? Do you remember me, even?" Cash masked it with a chuckle but he was thirsting to know how she remembered him exactly.

"I remember *you*," she said.

"What do you remember?"

"You were cute, you were nice. You knew a bunch of stuff about guitars."

Bullshit, he thought. *She remembers how Liam was with me.*

"You thought I was cute?" He grinned his most wolfish grin and looked sideways at her.

"Yeah, THOUGHT. Past tense," she teased back. She peaked at him out of the hood. Her hair was so long it came out of the front of the hood in a cascade of ebony.

They were quiet for a moment, just listening to the song. Finally they were next in line.

"I never forgot what you did for me," Cash said softly.

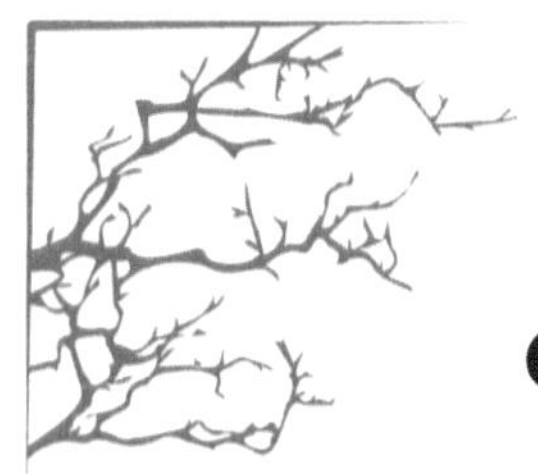

Chapter 25

Lila pulled her hood off and looked at him. Just then he pulled forward to the speaker.

Cash placed his order. Lila shifted uncomfortably. He couldn't possibly mean what she thought he meant. How could he have known?

"First of all, what are you referring to, sir?"

He shot her a disbelieving look.

"You know what I mean. With Liam. Freshman year."

"I dunno what you're talking about," she murmured, looking out the passenger window at nothing.

"I'm not trying to make you feel weird. I'm just saying. Liam made my life hell in junior high and then a few months into freshman year, you start going out with him. And from then on he left me alone."

"Hey. Hang on." Lila scooted up. "You're a fucking werewolf, why did you let him bully you? Why didn't you just like, go Wolverine on him?"

"I didn't start turning until senior prom," Cash said sheepishly.

Lila nodded.

"Timing is a bitch."

They pulled up to the window. Cash got his bag and pulled out. He set the warm bag on his lap and headed out to the hills above town.

"I like to go out to this one spot and look at the lights," he said.

They drove in silence, southeast and uphill, until they reached a remote turnout that had a clear view of the whole town.

"It's so much bigger than when I lived here," Lila remarked.

"You don't want to talk about Liam?"

She looked at him for a long moment.

"I didn't go out with Liam just to help you, if that's what you think."

"No! No. I just figured, I dunno, you put in a good word."

Lila was lying. She had dated Liam to get him to leave Cash alone. The three of them had detention together all the time, and she saw how Liam picked on him. He called him ugly names, made fun of his hair, just totally cartoonish.

It made her curious just how stupid Liam was, how deep the cruelty ran.

After detention let out one day, she cast Liam a look over her shoulder as she left. That was all it took, he did the rest, pursuing her with what she later learned was the confidence common to the below average.

One night, at the park that lay halfway between their houses, when she had her hand down his jeans, she said she thought it was loserish how he went in on Cash.

"You're way better than him. Why rub it in?"

He grunted, his clammy hand sliding up her top. But he pointedly didn't make fun of Cash in detention the next time they were all there.

"Why DID you date him?"

Lila sighed. She couldn't quite put it into words. The self destructiveness that she had decided to use to help someone else, for once.

"I wasn't super picky back then."

"Really? You turned me down," Cash said.

Lila raised her eyebrow.

"You were too nice for me. I would have made you do all sorts of awful things," she said with over the top wistfulness.

"Hey, I wasn't that nice. I got into trouble."

"Not the kind of trouble I would have given you."

Cash took a bite of his chalupa to avoid talking. Lila chewed her lip. By the time Cash had approached her, Lila had been hearing rumors about herself around school for three years. She stopped going out with high school boys at all, and snapped like a viper at anyone who approached her. But now, she was starting to think Cash hadn't ever heard the same rumors. Maybe he had talked to her from genuine interest. Not just to find out if what they said was true.

"At least, you know, if I remember right, I let you down gentle."

"Is that what you remember?" he chuckled.

"What?"

"I said, hey, can I have your number so I can ask you out some time?"

"Okay, and what did I say?"

"You didn't even look at me, you said, you aren't gonna ask me out. And you got up and walked away."

Lila folded in half in exaggerated shame.

"I guess compared to how you were with other people that wasn't so bad. You're right."

She groan-sighed.

"You told Damian you fucked his dad."

"Which one was Damian?"

"And you told him his dad said 'he worries about you because your dick is so small,'" lolllll this whole conversation is so funny Cash finished.

Lila smirked.

"Oh yeah. Damian just didn't have what it takes to thrive in this fast paced environment."

Cash rolled his eyes and started packing up his trash.

"I didn't really fuck his dad. I wasn't into dads. Just poetry majors from junior college," she said, after a brief pause.

"Hey, none of my beeswax. Fuck all the dads you want."

Something in his voice gave her pause. She turned to him, leaning her back against the truck's door.

"You don't know, do you?"

He looked at her.

"I never went out with the guys at school because there were about a million rumors where I had to get cum pumped out of my stomach and bit a guy's dick off in a car accident because I was giving him head. Any time I hung out with a boy from school it would be like, countdown to blowjob. So I just stopped."

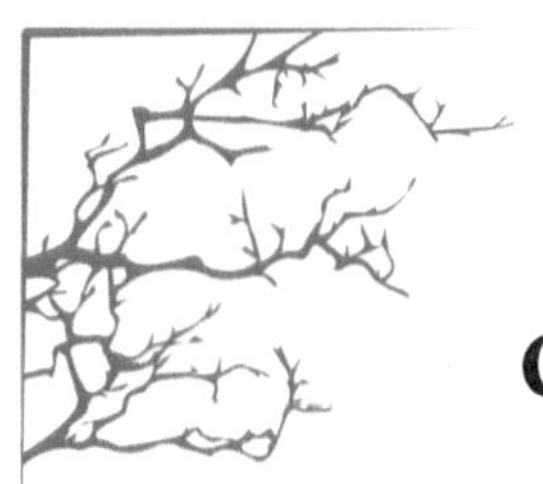

Chapter 26

Rage flared across Cash's features.

"I changed my mind. You can't eat Liam because I'm going to."

Lila grinned. A warm little ball formed in her tummy, and that feeling of safety settled over her again.

She smiled at him, and warmth burst in his chest. It was like starlight was trapped in her mouth. She squeezed his forearm, the one hanging on to the gear shift. He met her eyes and felt his own glowing, matching the predatory luminosity he suddenly saw in hers. He leaned towards her, and she towards him, a fraction of an inch. The air in the cab of the truck went electric, invisible currents arcing along their gazes.

Lila gasped and pulled away just as he did. He caught a glimpse of emotion flash across her face. Then it was gone. He looked away and sucked in a deep breath.

Cash started up the truck.

"I'm not trying to food shame you but how much do you actually consume?" she asked, shifting away from him and giving herself a little shake.

"I have an accelerated metabolism. Thanks for noticing," Cash confirmed. Lila giggled.

"So do you think I could booby trap the house with wooden stakes, Home Alone style? Or maybe pit traps, that might be better. How high can Emil jump?"

"You want to build boobie traps?"

"Yeah, you got any ideas?"

Strange how fast it was a routine with Lila - heading back to his house together. So far they had both been reacting to circumstances, but in this moment they hit a little patch of normalcy. A glimpse of what it would be like outside survival mode. They drove the rest of the way back to his house in companionable silence, windows down and radio on.

"Oh, it's Carolina. I'll be in in a sec," Cash said, picking up his phone after parking in the car port. Lila went inside.

"Hey."

"Hey."

The pause was tense.

"What's the deal with you and Lila? She's crashing at your house?" Carolina sounded more than annoyed. She sounded angry.

"I'm just helping her get back on her feet," Cash explained.

"Okay because you blew me off on Saturday to hang out with her, and then you sat there while she took some other guy out to the parking lot at the Acorn."

Cash cocked his head.

"We're just friends, Caro. And that wasn't what...ever you think it was."

"You ditched me for her and you're just friends? That's even worse."

He had no response.

"Don't be a sucker, Cash. I mean do you even know for sure she's done with her ex?"

"That's just about the one thing I'm sure of," he said grimly.

"I'm just looking out for you. I don't want her to hurt you again," Carolina said.

"I"m sorry I blew you off. I -"

"It doesn't matter, I don't need to hear some excuse. I'll still be here when she's gone. I just don't want you to get hurt."

"Got it." He didn't try to soften his tone. Carolina's words stung.

"Okay, well, I'll let you go."

Agitated, Cash shoved his phone in his pocket. He didn't know how to reassure Carolina without explaining about Lila. And what's more, it wouldn't even help. He was being stupid. He was falling for her, super fast and with reckless abandon for his heart. Hopefully this time Caro would be wrong.

"I have to get to sleep pretty soon. You want to watch a movie?" Cash suggested.

Lila shrugged agreeably. She curled up in the corner of the couch with the softest blanket.

Cash cued up Lord of the Rings.

"Wow. Nerd," Lila teased.

"It's without rival as far as sleep aids go," Cash countered.

Bowl of mixed nuts obtained, Cash sat against the arm of the couch, so his feet were towards Lila, and clicked play.

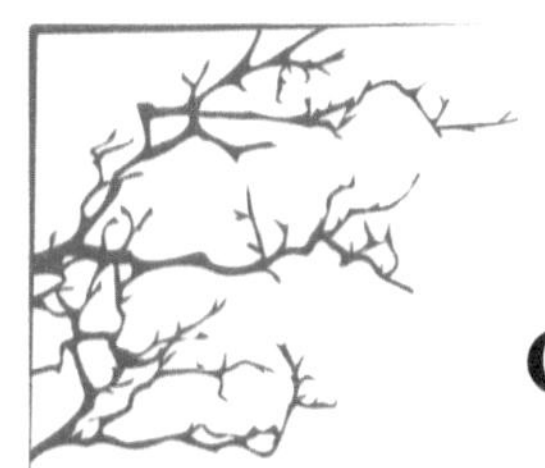

Chapter 27

Lila curled deeper into the couch. She was completely enveloped in Cash's scent, and she had never felt more safe.

Knowing that he knew she had done him that favor of sorts took the pressure off the arrangement. He was helping to pay her back. She wouldn't owe him.

She wrapped the blanket tighter around her, and a fresh wave of wolfy woodiness drifted over her. Emil would never be able to track her scent with this aura of lupine essence around her. She wanted to burrow into Cash's life and never leave.

"Are you cold? C'mere," Cash murmured. He gestured for her to move closer, so she did, even though she wasn't cold and couldn't feel cold. He sat up a little so both their legs could fit on the couch, and threw his arm over the back. Lila nuzzled under his armpit. His heart thumped steadily in her ear, but she forced down the thirst it aroused.

He was so warm it was heavenly. Lila, having no heartbeat, was basically cold blooded. Cash's body temperature was higher than most humans. She sighed. This whole situation wasn't ideal but it could be a lot worse. Cash could be a lot worse. Hopefully he tolerated her long enough for her to figure out how to get Emil off her case, and hopefully maybe even longer after that. She couldn't think too much farther ahead than saving her ass right now. All she knew was the idea of not seeing him again was intolerable.

Cash shifted slightly, terrified of disturbing Lila. She was laying against his side like a delicate baby bird, the blankets all tucked around her. His heart was pounding like crazy. Oh god, what if he still smelled like work, or worse, *TACO BELL*.

She was so soft. Her curves against his ribs and his hip. He could smell her hair, that rotten lily scent. It should have disgusted him but it drove him wild.

Wizards and hobbits could not hold his attention right now. He felt himself thickening against his stiff work jeans. He swallowed and shifted, trying to get comfortable. The more he moved, the worse he made it.

"Hey, sorry, I gotta go to bed," he mumbled.

Lila sat up, and her hood fell back. Her hair was all mussed. Cash wanted to smooth it so bad he had to restrain himself by clenching his fists.

"Okay. I'll finish this if it won't bother you?"

"Oh, who's the nerd now?" Cash winked. Lila scooched up, rolling her eyes at him.

He got up awkwardly, trying to keep his situation from being too obvious. He was sure Lila saw, though, with her perfect night vision.

Lila watched the movie with the sound off, reading the subtitles and listening to Cash shower. She was still so warm from his body heat, and swaddled in blankets that smelled like him. Her thighs pressed together, the gusset of her leggings dampening. The bulge in his jeans wouldn't get out of her head.

This wasn't right. She couldn't subject Cash to the danger of being around her, any more than she already was. If Emil knew they were anything, he would hurt Cash to hurt her. She had to stay away from him.

When Lila had tidied up Cash's room, she learned a lot about him. He had tons of little souvenir-like objects, with backstories she could only guess at. A one inch by one inch plush goldfish. A hollow ceramic cat. A pearl-handled buck knife.

Lila had never been one to hold onto objects. She wasn't sentimental about stuff, because growing up anything she had, she would be forced to share with her half brother Colin. Her dad, stepmom, and Colin moved to Texas on Lila's eighteenth birthday, leaving Lila in Lawry with only her ten-year-old car and a suitcase of clothes. Lila had left for Los Angeles a week later. Why stay in Lawry? She'd always hated it.

For the first year in LA, she'd been too poor to have anything just to have it. She lived in a hostel, then briefly a homeless shelter, all while doing gig work.

June of her second summer in Hollywood, her car broke down on the 405 at ten pm while she was trying to deliver someone's pad Thai. Steam was pouring out of the engine and smoke from the tailpipe. She had pulled over and broken down herself, sobbing in frustration at how fucking hard life had to be.

That's when Sasha pulled over in her black '62 Lincoln.

"Need some help, sweetheart?"

After that Lila hadn't had anything of her own because everything of hers belonged to Emil. So she had no childhood keepsakes. Cash had dozens. His family must love him so much.

He had tons of books, too, and magazines about electronics. Crates of records of bands she'd never heard of. That's when she found the over-ear headphones and started listening.

At first the metal records had seemed either silly or incomprehensibly growly. But the more she listened to, the more she liked it. The high energy was the opposite of the grim, dirge-like atmosphere at the mansion. The lyrics were about mass murderers and war but the overall effect was uplifting. It was exactly like Cash - kinda scary looking, with his scowl and his denim and black wardrobe. But his heart was pure as sunshine. He was kind and a good friend. And he was protecting her. Whatever his reason, he was risking his life to protect her.

The movie was over but Lila wasn't ready to sleep. She decided to keep her hands busy by cleaning the kitchen. It felt strange but good to do something with her hands. At the mansion, Emil's little human underlings did all the cleaning.

Busy though her hands were, her mind was busier. Emil was still in Northern California. She was sure of it, like sensing rain in the atmosphere. It was only a matter of time. She had to figure out how to stop him before he found her. Before he found Cash.

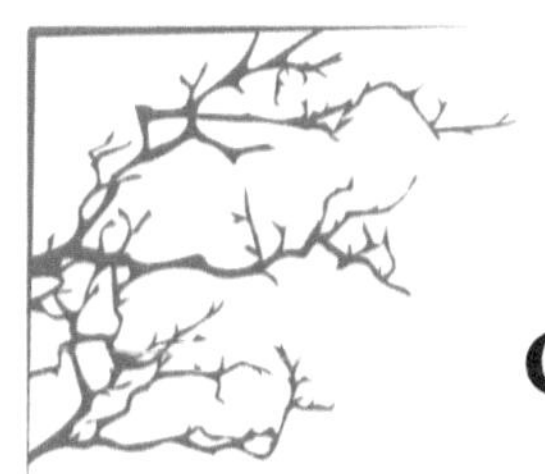

Chapter 28

Cash lay awake in his pitch black bedroom. He had foolishly checked his clock and discovered it was still an hour until he could justify getting out of bed. No hope of falling back asleep.

Lila was up, he could hear her moving around. This room may be light proof but it was not sound proof, especially not for a werewolf.

Was she cleaning the kitchen? She seemed to feel she owed him. He didn't feel she had anything to make up for, but she was sure of it.

He was in deep trouble with her. It wasn't like Carolina thought, that he was trying to get a do-over. He saw something in Lila. The desire to be a better person. Plus she was funny. Plus she was so soft and cuddly and smelled so good.

Not wanting to intrude on Lila's awake time, he rolled over and tried to lull himself to sleep by picturing himself walking along the blueprint for the jobsite in San Simon. Tracing every wall and joist from a bird's eye view, locating every wall socket and switchboard, until his eyes got heavy and...

He jerked awake again.

Cash flipped onto his back and put his hands behind his head. What if Carolina was right? And Carter, for that matter.

What if Lila was lying, or tricking him? Maybe she could tell he was lonely and saw him as an easy mark.

That could be the case with any new person I might date, though, he logicked. *But most of them wouldn't be undead blood suckers.*

He heard the kitchen tap shut off, the nearly imperceptible steps of a vampire approaching, and velcro ripping open.

Lila slipped through the door.

"Hey," he muttered.

"Hey."

She unzipped his hoodie and laid it over the back of his chair. Cash studiously looked away as she stripped off her leggings, but Lila didn't hide herself. She climbed into bed in just an undershirt of his, long on her but covering everything by the skin of its teeth, and got under the covers.

Is she doing this on purpose? Teasing me for getting hard like a teenager? She fuckin makes me feel like a teenager -

"Did I wake you?" she asked softly, interrupting his lust-addled thoughts.

"I was already awake," he said.

She was lying on her side, facing him, her hands under her cheek like a cherub. The curves of her waist and breasts showed under the clinging white shirt. The sight of her made him flustered.

He turned to mirror her. Lila got lost in his eyes, the lashes soft like black feathers, and realized she was staring without speaking.

"I like your metal records," she said.

"You do?" He gave her a little smile.

"Yeah. I listened to a bunch of them the other day."

Her pinky traced little patterns on the fitted sheet.

"Which ones did you particularly like?" he asked. He let his hand slip out to rest on the sheet between them, near hers. Her fingers were slender with pointed nails, claws really.

"I liked Power Trip. And I liked Blind Guardian."

"Two of my favorites as well," he agreed. Her pinky slid across the sheet and came to a rest just touching his. He scooted her hand closer, so their whole sides were touching. In response, she pressed her fingers closer.

Cash placed his palm on the back of her hand and interlaced their fingers.

The air got very heavy. He looked up at her. Her eyes were bright again, but not like in the truck before. She licked her bottom lip and took a little breath.

He leaned into her space and met her lips with his. Her mouth, her skin, were so soft, and cool to the touch.

Her hand slipped out from under his and caressed up his bicep, along his shoulder, making him shiver with anticipation. He deepened their kiss and moved his hand to her waist, her soft little waist. This was so good, and he wanted more, so much more. He rubbed her skin through the fabric and she wrapped her fingers around the back of his neck. Her tongue was cool, too, and he felt her sharp fangs trace along his lip as they explored each other's mouths.

Cash moved closer, so their knees were touching. He wanted to climb on top of her and claim her, body and soul. The wolf in him was clawing at him, trying to take over. His human brain told him to move slow.

He pulled back a little to get some air. She gasped and blinked hard.

"Did I scare you?" he asked, worried by her expression.

"Scare me?" she whispered.

"You're not afraid I'll hurt you?"

"Nothing you could do could harm me," she said. "I'm more scared of hurting you."

"*Me?*" He was genuinely confused.

"When we're close I can hear your blood rushing in your veins. I can feel your heartbeat. You're so fucking *alive*," she said, her brow furrowed. "I can't tell if I'm going to lose it and rip your throat open."

"I could do the same to you."

She shook her head. His fingers danced on her hip.

"Ever since I started changing, I haven't..." he began.

"What?"

"I haven't wanted to be with anyone. Because I don't know if I'm going to hurt them. Strong feelings and sensations, like, trigger it, sometimes."

"You could change during sex?"

"Well that's the nightmare scenario, I guess. That I wouldn't be able to distract my senses and the wolf would come out."

She considered.

"I dunno. That could be kind of hot," Lila said, without a hint of sarcasm.

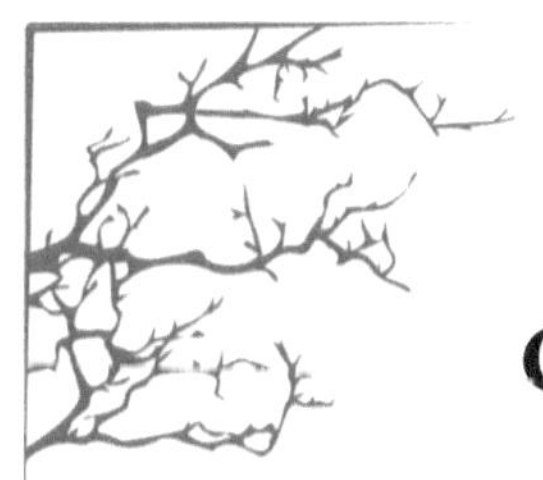

Chapter 29

Her hand was resting on Cash's chest and she felt his heart start to speed up again when she said that.

"*Hot?*"

"I saw what you look like after you switch. It's not, like, an actual animal. You're like, still human."

"Are you telling me you want to... to fuck my werewolf form?" The wildness inside him bucked up at that, wanting to bust free.

"No! I dunno! I just... I'm just saying it wouldn't be *my* nightmare scenario."

"But *you* biting *me*, that's a nightmare. Because my blood is so disgusting."

"NO. Because I could lose it and kill you. I have no idea what werewolf blood will do to me. What if it makes me like hyper vampiric?"

"Have you ever lost it and killed someone before?"

"I mean, it's been kind of close but... no. Have you?"

Images of the fight he'd been in at 21 with one of his former bullies came to mind. But even then he'd reined it in.

"No."

They looked at each other, not speaking, for two long breaths. Then he reached for her as she pulled him to her. Their bodies met in the middle and his arms wound around Lila, one hand buried in her hair and the other landing on the small of her back.

Her mouth opened for his, her lips full and soft and her tongue licking at him. Her hand went under the covers, tracing along his ribs to his hip, her touch chilling his blazing skin.

Lila breathed hard, her eyes rolling back as she forced her fangs not to puncture Cash's tongue and lips. She could taste his life as he kissed her, could feel his pulse in her mouth. Her sex throbbed wet and hot at his touch, and the two needs pushed her forward.

She threw her leg over his thigh, and he instantly bucked into her, his erection hot through his underwear. She released his mouth and gasped, and he kissed down her throat, his hand in her hair tugging her head back.

Her heel dug into the back of his thigh, spurring him to grind against her.

Cash grabbed her hip and shifted her so he was above her, resting her hips in his lap and her thighs on his. Her shirt rucked up, and she squirmed so her damp core rubbed him.

He rested his hands on either side of her and bent to kiss her neck, her collarbone, her ear. She panted and ran her hands up his bare sides, rocking her hips against him. God, she was fucking eager. His cock was hard as stone and leaking already. He wanted to take his time, though. When he thought of how tenuous this all was - he didn't want to waste it.

"You're so fucking beautiful," he whispered, staring at her porcelain face in the faint red glow from his clock radio.

She shook her head, overwhelmed, and her gleaming black hair fanned out around her. Cash caressed her cheek and held her little chin in his big hand. He kissed her softly, his lips warm and gentle. Working down, he pressed wet lips to her pulseless throat. His hand slid up under her shirt, and traced along her ribs. She shuddered, and he grazed the curve of her breast with his thumb, looking up at her face to check her reaction. She whined, clutching at his shoulders, so he brushed her nipple with his thumb and she bucked into him, grinding herself on his cock. His fingers danced on her skin.

"Fuck," he whispered huskily. She threw her head back in apparent frustration.

"Cash," she squeaked. He was teasing her, and she was going nuts. She was soaked aching for more. And he had barely touched her.

He rolled her nipple in his fingers, and rocked his hips into her. She moaned softly, arching into him.

"I want to taste you," he said, his mouth hot on her chest. She nodded her assent and he pushed the tank top up her torso, baring her full breasts and pebbled nipples to the air. He bent his head to her and took her in his mouth, licking and squeezing her flesh. A continuous babble of panting moans spilled from her lips and her hands clutched at his shoulders.

His chest rested on her tummy, and the sensation of his hair rubbing her velvety skin stirred something animal and hungry in her.

He moved down, his lips kissing a trail down the center of her ribs to her bellybutton. Her insides clenched with each kiss, the tension making her writhe.

When he reached the crest of her thighs, he ran his finger along her mound, not touching where she most wanted him. He took a moment to collect himself. Her scent was heady in the air, all around him, making him drunk with it. He looked up at her.

Her bottom lip was between her teeth, her shiny white fangs pressing dents in the gleaming ruby skin. The pleading in her eyes urged him on, and he dipped his thumb to caress the apex of her slit. He lifted her legs up to his shoulders and settled between them.

Cash ran his palms up her smooth, cool legs. He knelt in front of her with her ankles on his shoulder. His cock was throbbing, begging to be touched, but he ignored it and kissed across her stomach to just above her mound. She whined and squirmed again. He loved that sound. She was so eager for him it was making him cocky - he was forgetting that he hadn't done this in four years.

"Cash," she whispered, "Please."

That was all he needed to hear. He pressed his lips to her mound, kissing the little tuft of hair there, nuzzling it with his nose. His stubble scraped her deliciously as he nuzzled lower, til his lips found the crest of her, and he kissed it delicately. Little licks with the tip of his tongue at first, then moving stronger and faster as her panting moans told him what worked. He cupped her ass with one massive hand while the other found her entrance, his fingers slowly working into her.

Lila panted, her heels digging into his upper back. Her walls constricted around his knuckles and her hands gripped his shoulders. He slipped another finger in, curling to stroke the spot that made her muscles seize.

She cried out as she reached her peak, her juices washing over his hand. He lapped them up like healing waters, easing her through her climax.

"Fuck," she whimpered, as he kissed up her stomach. His stubble grazed her skin, all the way up her neck. She grabbed his face and pressed her lips to his, her tongue winding into his mouth.

"Want you so bad," he growled. His hardness pressed against her damp center through his briefs, She nodded, beyond words. The sound of his pulse thudded in Lila's ears and she licked the points of her fangs. Her fists gripped the sheets as Cash rustled in his bedside table. He pulled out a shiny packet and opened it. She watched as he pulled his briefs down and his cock sprung free.

"Christ," she gasped. "Is it even gonna fit?"

Cash's face flushed and he rolled the rubber down his length. Lila reached for him, pulling him down to face her. Her thighs bowed around his hips, and he reached down to guide himself into her.

Lila threw her head back, baring her pearly throat to Cash. He filled her, slowly, giving them both time to adjust. When he was as deep as he could go, he dropped his forehead to hers.

"Give me a sec," he murmured. The way this felt, he wasn't sure how long he could last. Lila nodded, running her hands up and down his ropey biceps and delts. When the little eleven between her brows loosened, and he felt her hips rock under his, he started to move. Slowly at first, savoring her. Lila arched her back, and Cash took his cue to thrust harder. He leaned on one elbow and slipped his thumb between them, finding her clit.

Lila's hands went to the back of his neck. He bent to kiss her, working her every nerve in a symphony. She began to chant his name, clutching him harder and harder until he felt her spasming around him on a sobbing moan.

He spilled into the condom as she came, babbling into her ear.

"You're so fucking beautiful, you feel so fucking good."

She wrapped her calves around his lower back and pulled him even deeper into her. He shuddered, hypersensitive.

Cash withdrew gently to dispose of the condom and get a clean tee shirt. He kissed Lila's cheeks and eyelids as he cleaned her up, and then threw the tee shirt in his hamper.

He got back between the sheets and Lila cozied up under his armpit, her head on his shoulder. He savored her legs tangling with his.

"Wow," she sighed. He chuckled. She traced nonsense patterns in the curly hair on his chest and solar plexus. He wanted to wrap himself around her like a bullet proof vest.

"Do you really have to go to work?" Lila asked.

"Yeah. Pretty soon, too. I was late yesterday."

She sighed dramatically and snuggled deeper into his side.

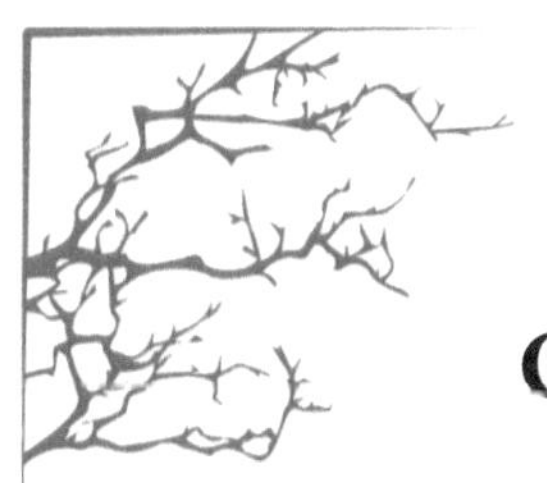

Chapter 30

Cash tried not to think about what just happened and what it would mean. His heart felt a size too big for his chest. He swallowed.

"I should get up. Tonight when I get home I'll install some cameras. You'll, um, you'll be okay while I'm gone?"

She looked up at him. His eyes searched hers, but he couldn't tell what she was thinking.

"I'll be snug as a bug in a rug," she said.

Reluctantly, Cash dragged himself out of bed to get ready for work. Sleepy and sated, Lila watched him dress, running her hand over the warm spot he had left.

Cash tugged on clean undies and jeans, feeling unusually conscious of his nudity. He hadn't been naked in front of a lady since shortly after high school. Four long years ago.

He zipped up and turned back around as he tucked his pockets in. Lila was all curled up in the center of the bed, like a fox kit, her face more at peace than he'd seen her. Her lips had softened into a gentle smile. The sight of her safe and warm in his bed stirred him, man and beast alike. If only he could climb back into her arms and show her why she should never leave.

His cock woke back up at the thought. If he didn't hustle, he'd be late again.

He growled and pulled on a tee shirt. Later.

Lila snuggled deep into the covers. The front door clicked shut, and Cash's truck started. She basked in the luxury of this safe haven. Somehow, Cash was willing to risk his neck and his heart by letting her invade his life this way. She felt so lucky.

If she'd met him back in LA, at the beginning with Sasha when it still felt like the kinds of sleepovers she'd never been invited to as a kid, she would have gushed to Sasha about Cash. How thoughtful he was. How he didn't even care about her reputation at Lawry High. No more than she cared about his rep for being a nerd virgin.

Sasha would press for steamy details and Lila would spill that she had lost count of the orgasms.

Except, Sasha would have been disgusted, because Cash was a werewolf. How ridiculous. Maybe the LA vampires had never met a shifter - or maybe other shifters weren't like Cash. She stuffed her nose in his pillow to breathe his not-at-all-dirty scent, to which she was starting to get hooked.

Lila's thoughts swirled chaotically. She hadn't been expecting to catch feelings on her way through town. And the longer she stayed here the more danger Cash was in. But how could she possibly leave now?

It was delusional to believe that some security cameras and his wolfiness would keep Emil away forever. And knowing Cash little though she did, she suspected he was wildly protective of people he cared about. Which she seemed to be, despite his own best interests.

It would be for the best if she sat him down tonight and broke it down. She needed to leave town, not by choice but for his own safety. She needed to leave this incredibly den of coziness and warmth and yummy smells.

Lila sighed deep into Cash's pillow and tried not to cry.

Spencer was already at the coffee place when Cash pulled up. His office was around the corner in historic downtown Lawry.

"They're making our stuff," he said as Cash walked up.

"Aw, you got it last time," Cash groused.

"Dude! We're celebrating."

"Yeah? Why's that?" Cash cocked his head at Spencer, wondering if his bestie had somehow gleaned his own good turn of events.

"Melissa and I are officially exclusive," Spencer beamed. The barista handed him two large drinks, and he passed one to Cash, then clinked the lids like they were toasting.

"Congrats, dude," Cash said. They walked outside. Cash felt gangly and in the way inside those places.

"She's the smartest girl I ever dated for sure. She's a nurse practitioner. That's like, a real job."

"Yeah, she seems nice."

Cash barely remembered Melissa - meeting her had felt like a year ago even though it was only a week.

"Yeah, I think we're gonna go to El Greco tonight if you want to meet up."

"Oh, that would be awesome. Maybe later on. Lila might -"

"Dude! She's still here?"

Cash nodded.

"And still like... drinking blood and shit?" Spencer asked, leaning in to lower his voice.

"Uh... yeah," Cash said. He sipped his coffee.

"Lotta cream lotta sugar right?"

"Yeah. You got it," Cash smiled. Spencer really was the most thoughtful.

"So what's going on with that? Are you two hooking up? How long's she in Lawry?"

Cash put his sunglasses on.

"I don't know. We're not... not hooking up."

Spencer hooted.

"Shut up," Cash snapped. "Just... shut up."

"Okay okay. It's not a thing for sure yet. Anyway she's still crashing at the house though?"

"Yeah. I don't know for how long. Listen, she's trying to avoid her ex. So I'm not, like, gonna take her on double dates or whatever."

"Oh for sure for sure. Cool dude, I'm gonna go to work now but thanks for meeting up, I just wanted to share the good news."

"Right on. Congrats," Cash said, and they clapped each other's shoulders goodbye.

Cash turned on Carolina's show as he did every morning. Her voice over the air just reminded him of her words. That Lila was only going to hurt him. He felt like an idiot because he didn't care. Maybe she would hurt him. The risk was worth it. He couldn't wait to get through this day and go back to her.

They could figure everything out. Even Emil. It would be worth it. He thought of her hands on his back, her breath on his skin. All he wanted was to hold her and protect her and feed her. Carolina would come around. So would Carter. They would see that despite her history and what she was, she was good inside.

A flash of light woke Lila. She threw the covers over her head in pure terror, but quickly realized the flash had been a dream. A dream she was still in. Inside a car, on the road into Lawry.

Lila snapped her eyes open and scrambled up into a sitting position. Emil was here. He was almost here. How long until he found Cash's house? Surely not long at all. Was he tracking her scent? She began to breathe harder, and tears pricked her eyes.

The glowing red face of the clock radio read four thirty PM. Cash would be back soon, she thought. Didn't construction sites close up at five? Sunset would be at six. Shit. She was trapped here, inside this room. And she had no way to get ahold of Cash and warn him.

She began to breathe harder, and spots danced in front of her eyes. She didn't know what to do.

Cursing herself for staying here all this time and putting Cash in harm's way, she wrapped herself up in his dirty clothes and hid in the closet. If she was lucky both Cash and nightfall would arrive before Emil, and she could warn him and bolt. Try to draw Emil away. Until then all she could do was try to mask her scent and hide.

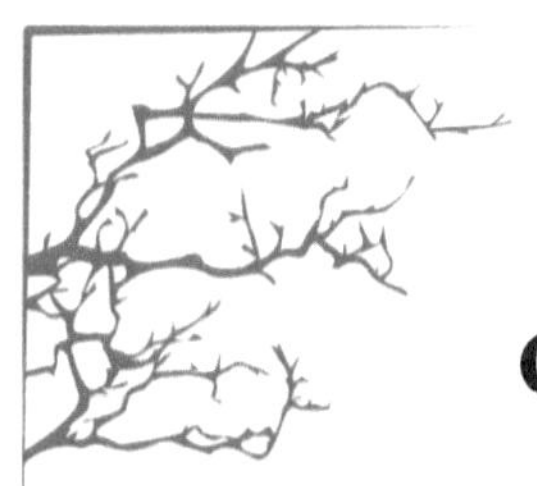

Chapter 31

When Cash got back into Lawry, something immediately felt off. A scent, a magnetic shift. The air was strange.

He sped through town, taking all the shortcuts he knew to get back to his place fast.

He pulled off the main road and parked his truck at the produce stand on the corner. He wanted to approach his house silently. Someone was here, and it could only be Emil.

Fuck it, he thought, and let his bestial form come tearing out of him. He shook all over, fur and ears settling into place, and began to circle around to his back door, moving on two feet. Dusk was beginning to fall and his lupine eyes adjusted to the low light, picking up the most minute movements around him. His ears swiveled uselessly - vampires could move as quietly as mist. *Like owls,* he thought, and then the scent of dead blood overwhelmed him like chloroform, and an arm like an iron bar went around his throat.

Lila heard noises outside. She flung Cash's clothes off her and smashed the closet door open, pushing it off its tracks by mistake. The room was dark and the clock read six fifteen. She rushed out of the bedroom and into the living room.

"Cash?"

LILAAA

She fell to her knees as Emil's voice filled her mind.

"Show yourself you demonic piece of shit!" she hollered.

I'M RIGHT HERE, DARLING he hissed.

He landed on the back stoop, boots heavy on the planks. He had Cash, in his wolf form, in a chokehold, and his green eyes were like toxic waste. He must have literally just fed.

"I'm not letting you in, asshole," Cash coughed. Emil began to levitate, rising just high enough so Cash had to stand on tip toes to keep from choking. Cash clawed at his arm but the wounds healed over as fast as he slashed them.

"Emil, let him go," Lila yelled. "You don't want him."

Emil's eyes were wild, and she had no idea what he would do next.

NO, I DON'T. UNLIKE YOU I DON'T LUST AFTER ANIMALS.

Lila scowled. The sound of him inside her skull was metallic, shrill.

IF YOU COME WITH ME I WON'T SLIT HIS THROAT

His serpentine tongue flicked out.

Cash struggled harder, thrashing in Emil's steely grip.

IT'S YOUR CHOICE.

"Lila, no! Don't do it," Cash choked out. But Lila was already crossing the room, flinging open the sliding glass door, wrenching Emil's ropey forearm off Cash's neck. She pushed Emil backwards, summoning her strength to get him further from Cash.

Meanwhile, Cash spun around, bounding off the stoop claws-out at Emil.

Emil backhanded him mid-pounce, throwing Cash off his feet. Cash landed on his back and scrambled backwards, his tail swishing.

"Cash, don't. He'll kill you," Lila cried. She turned to her former captor. "I'll go with you, Emil. It's fine. Just leave him alone."

She turned back to Cash who had gotten back to his feet.

"Thank you for everything. Goodbye. Don't come after me," she said, with an empty finality that crushed Cash's heart into dust.

Emil, now earthbound, grasped Lila's arm.

YOU BELONG WITH ME. I MADE YOU.

She shut her eyes, and went along as Emil dragged her around to the front of the house.

Cash heard a car pull up, and the doors open and shut. He ran around the house in time to see a black town car with tinted windows pulling away on the gravel.

He threw his silver head back and howled all his frustration and rage.

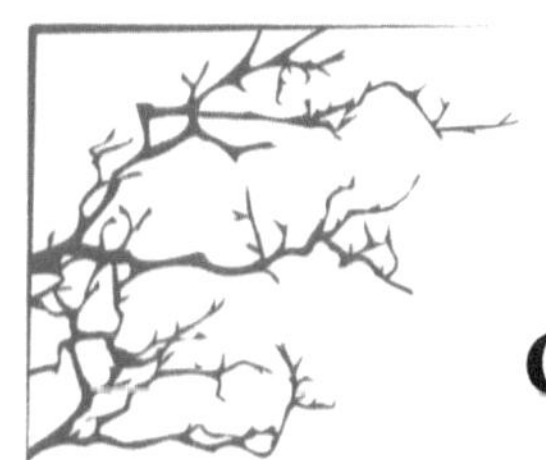

Chapter 32

The back of the town car was comfortable enough. Lila sat obediently across from Emil. She stared out the window at the black night landscape rushing by. Cody, Emil's human pet, had his foot to the floor as he drove them down the interstate towards Los Angeles. He had puncture wounds on his neck and hands. So he'd been feeding Emil on this little road trip. How convenient.

Emil had his feet up on the center console, his body sprawled across the back seat. Lila couldn't stand to look at him.

"Did you have fun on your little adventure, puppet?"

Lila didn't respond. Emil pushed her thigh with his bare foot. A two hundred year old vampire and he acted like a child most of the time. Lila hated him with her entire being.

Head turned to the window, she bit down on her knuckle to keep from crying. Of course it was stupid to think she and Cash could work. That she could stay in Lawry, be free from Emil. Be happy. Since she was born she'd been unwanted, her father and stepmother making it clear she was a burden. Cash had actually wanted her there, for no reason other than he liked her. And it was impossible for her to stay with him.

Emil began to talk at her, telling her all the ways she was an idiot. How easy it had been to track her down. How horrible she smelled.

"I'll have to get this car deep cleaned. You smell like a kennel. If you were so unhappy, puppet, you could have said something. You didn't have to prove a point by bunking in an actual dog house."

Lila shook her head. He wasn't going to get in this time. Even if he tortured her she wouldn't be his anymore, not inside.

Uphill he ran, past the oaks and scrub into the redwoods. Cash ran hard and fast, the foliage flowing past him. He was fueled by rage and heartbreak.

Far up into the Balenas mountains, out where he sometimes saw mountain lions, Cash finally slowed to a stop in a clearing. The waning moon sat low in the sky, but Cash sat back on his haunches and howled anyway. He cried out all his frustration to her silver face.

Why couldn't I have just come home earlier?

He was so pissed at himself for getting ambushed. Lila was gone and he would never forgive himself for not protecting her.

She had only been here a few days. He knew his mother, and Carolina, and probably even Spencer, would tell him he was being a sucker. But he knew what he felt for Lila. He knew if they had a chance they could be good together. And now, that chance was impossible because he had been gone when she needed him.

A ragged edge came into his howl, a desperate plea. He would do whatever he had to to get her back.

THE CAR ARRIVED AT the Hollywood mansion an hour before dawn. With familiar dread, Lila followed Emil from the garage up the stairs into the house.

"Guess who's back, darling," he cackled while sauntering into the cavernous living room. Lila steeled herself to see Sasha and the others again. The loggia windows had been closed and covered with their two story light proof curtains. On the other side lay the pool with its wall of juniper trees, and beyond that a lawn that sloped uphill to the back of the lot. Before she had turned, Lila had liked to take a blanket out to that lawn and lay out in the sun, the pepper trees along the fence swaying in the wind.

"What's that STENCH?" Sasha caterwauled from the white leather couch. She was so dramatic. Lila had thought she was so funny and compelling at first. But now the over the top reactions to every little thing were tiresome.

Samson and Bruce didn't seem to be here. Probably out collecting victims. Or already in bed.

"She was staying with some werewolf! How disgusting!" Emil crowed. Lila didn't care if they spent the next fifty years making fun of her. They could say whatever they wanted. If she had to stay here with them, she would have to completely dissociate. Just being in the same room with Emil was barely tolerable. An eternity as his sycophant would be hell. Lila stretched her neck and shoulders. She was exhausted.

"Honestly. Your stink is getting on everything. Did your werewolf rub his asshole all over you?" Sasha sneered.

"It's too late to bathe so you'll have to sleep in the lower crypt," Emil tossed off. Lila shut her eyes.

"Okay." The lower crypt was an unfinished dirt basement with concrete walls. Bugs crawled over you when you slept in it. It didn't matter though. Nothing mattered. She was trapped here forever with these pricks.

CASH SHOULD HAVE TRIED to sleep after he transformed. Or maybe getting drunk as hell would have helped. All he knew was he was in no shape to sleep, or work, or do anything but pace around his house in his human form, thoughts a carousel of panic and rage.

He'd been so fucking stupid. First to fall for Lila at all. And second to put cameras on the house the day he moved in two years ago. At least then he would have known that Emil was there. Instead, big stupid wolf that he was, he had barged right into the trap and gotten Lila taken.

Cash slammed into his bedroom and grabbed clean clothes from the pile. Unsure what he was planning, he got in his truck and headed for the All Nite.

He slalomed into a parking space halfway across the parking lot. The morning sun struggled to break through the gray dome of the sky. Cash stomped inside.

He wasn't even sure what he was looking for. Was he going to buy a shotgun and shoot Emil with it? That wouldn't even work.

He wandered the aisles, picking things up and putting them down. Finally he grabbed a case of beer. There had been no reason to come to this store. He was just distracting himself however he could, so he didn't break something.

He needed to calm his nerves and distract his senses. The wolf in him was clawing to come out and run all the way to Los Angeles. All that would get him was killed, and probably Lila too.

"Cash? Dude."

He spun around to see Spencer holding a massive All Nite coffee.

"Spence!" He bent to hug him. Spencer glanced down at his thirty rack.

"Watcha... doin, there, buddy?"

"Lila's gone."

He stared at him.

"What happened?"

"He took her. Emil. Her ex took her."

Spencer's face instantly softened.

"Oh, no, I'm so sorry... wait but... Like he kidnapped her?"

Cash nodded.

"Fuck. Did you call the cops?"

Cash furrowed his brow.

"I don't know how I would explain this vampire shit to a cop."

Spencer pursed his lips.

"Right."

"I have to go down to LA and get her. I might have to kill her maker. I dunno. I know this is insane. And if she were a human it would be. But this isn't some big romantic win her back gesture thing. He's gonna kill her, or hurt her."

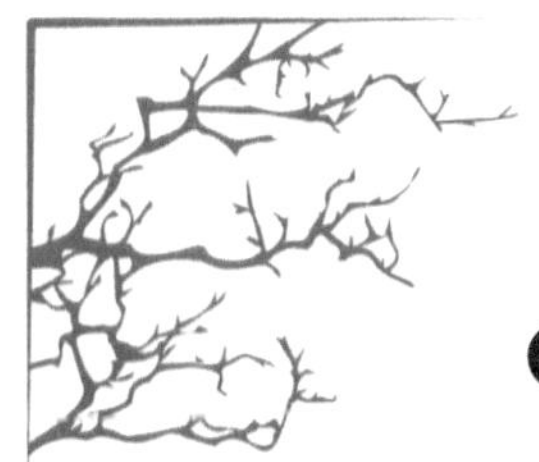

Chapter 33

Cash hadn't known that's what he was planning until it came out.

Spencer watched him for a beat.

"You still really care about her?"

"I care about her more than ever."

"Even if she doesn't... you know... even if it doesn't work out still?"

"Jesus Christ, Spence. I'm not some incel. I don't want her to die in torment, whether she wants to be with me or not."

"Okay okay sorry. I just gotta be protective of you, dude. You don't protect yourself for shit."

Inside the lower crypt the air was still and thick. Lila lay on her back, waiting for sleep that would not come. Instead thoughts of Cash, every moment of her knowing him, tormented her.

Cash across the quad, his hair bobbing above the heads of the others. So she always knew where he was.

Cash in the parking lot of the All Nite, waving hi to her with two fingers cocked while his thumbs rested in his pockets. He was watching Spencer try to chat up some semi-Alt girls. Lila herself had been there with her pseudo-boyfriend at the time, Figs, who had run inside to grab a liter of vodka for the college drama department party he was taking her to. Lila had stayed outside to smoke while leaning on his car.

She used to wear thick black eyeliner and oversized black hoodies atop a mini dress or black leggings. When people talked to her she would scowl at them. She had no friends her own age. So she mostly hung out at the coffee shop downtown, where she met guys like Figs.

Cash and Spencer had always been nice enough to her. Not sniggering nice like they were picturing what they just heard about her. Carolina, Lila couldn't remember if they had ever talked in high school.

The thing was, she wasn't just putting on a mean front. She was mean. She hated all the other kids at school, and she hated her family. Her rage boiled over in the form of razor sharp insults more often than not. Eventually most people started leaving her alone. Cash thought she had been rude when she turned him down, and maybe so, but a lot of other guys had gotten it worse.

That night outside the megamart, Cash glanced at Spencer and then strode over to where Lila leaned on Figs's dented sedan. She was about to light her next cigarette from the butt of her first, a habit she remembered people called "butt fucking." So charming.

Cash had flipped open his Zippo and lit her cigarette.

"What are you up to tonight?" he asked in his gritty baritone. He was wearing his denim vest, covered with illegible metal band patches, over a leather jacket.

"Party with Figs. You?"

He nodded.

"Cactus club with Spencer. Antarctic Legions is playing."

"You want a cigarette?" she offered.

"Nah. Only weed for me.

He hadn't looked away from her face. She studiously gazed towards the store's glowing fluorescent entrance.

"Which one is Figs? The trumpet player?"

"No. That's Anthony. Figs is the playwright."

"Oh, with the whole," Cash gestured like throwing a scarf over his shoulder. Lila snorted.

"Yeah. With the scarf."

Cash was enough of a coffee shop regular to know the characters and that Lila hung out there all the time.

"Here he comes now," she murmured, dropping her cigarette. "Thanks for the light."

Figs returned with his jug of spirits. He draped his arm over Lila's shoulder, which was awkward since he was barely the same height as her.

"Ready, Babe?" he asked, looking Cash up and down. Cash's eyebrow quirked up.

"Sure," Lila said, turning with him to get in the car. She looked back at Cash and rolled her eyes. He smiled and nodded goodbye.

Now Lila lay on a dirt floor in a stifling crypt, spider footsteps the only sound. The night might bring torture, death, or just boredom. She was reasonably certain she would never see Cash again, alive or dead, and that certainty is what finally made tears of blood stream from her eyes. She sobbed into her arm, hoping the others couldn't hear her in their caskets in the outer crypt.

Spencer came back to Cash's place with him. Cash put on a pot of strong coffee.

"So what's your plan when you get there? Do you know, like, exactly where you're going?"

"No. But I think I can find it. Lila said the house was in Beverly Hills and it was a white mansion with a glass wall. There can't be that many of those. So I'm gonna use the satellite map view and narrow it down. If I get close I'll be able to smell them, I'm pretty sure. I caught Lila's scent from like a mile away before."

"Dude, your eyes are doing that yellow thing right now."

Cash took a deep breath. His fangs were itching, too. He was on the verge of switching.

"Alright, don't judge me." He pulled a fifth of Laphroaig out of the cabinet, unscrewed the top and took a swig right out of the bottle. The smokey burn filled his mouth and made his eyes water. It was only ten AM. He felt his fangs recede.

"That actually works?"

Cash nodded.

"Other things do too, like smashing my thumb with a hammer, or spicy food. This way is the most pleasant."

He got his laptop from the bedroom. Lila's scent hung thickly in here, and he shook his head. How could he feel such grief when he'd had only a few days with her?

Plopping onto the couch, he flipped his computer open.

"I already found one that could be it," Spencer said. He air dropped a screenshot of a mansion to Cash. Cash pinned the location on his map app. The two men began the virtual hunt. The hyperfocus that had helped them beat video games and build guitars as kids returned and they were silent except for the occasional "Found one."

Cash wasn't sure how long they'd been looking when his phone buzzed. Carolina.

"Hey," she answered, softer than he expected.

"Hey! I just wanted to say I'm sorry that I was blowing you off. You're right. This whole thing has been crazy."

"Oh, no, I'm sorry. I shouldn't have said anything. I'm just protective. But you're a big boy. And I'm sure Lila's done with her ex."

Cash's stomach dropped.

"Well. Funny you should mention that."

"What?"

"Her ex kind of... kidnapped her."

"What the fuck? So he really is a total psycho?"

"Yeah like... beyond."

"Whoa. Is she okay? Have you heard from her?"

"No."

"Wait. Was she kidnapped or did she go back to him? Like really."

"No. I was there. He made her go with him. He was threatening to kill me."

"Okay because -"

"Caro. I know. I'm not being a sap, okay? She needs my help."

Carolina said nothing, for so long Cash thought she must have hung up.

"I trust you. How are you supposed to help her?"

"I have to go to LA. Spencer's helping me find the house."

Carolina sucked in a big breath and let it out.

"Okay. Are you gonna be safe?"

"I'm gonna try."

By three they had searched every street within the city of Beverly Hills, hunting down white mansions. They had maps with red dots all over it - places where Lila could be.

Cash was stiff and grouchy from hunching over his computer. And he was starving.

"I'm gonna pack up then hit up Golden West on the way out of town," Cash said, turning to Spencer.

"Been thinking about it a lot. I'm gonna come with you."

"What? Absolutely not."

"Yeah. I definitely am. Because you're gonna need someone to help you find this place and stake it out. No pun intended."

"Spencer. I appreciate it. But there is no way I'm bringing you to a vampire nest. I wouldn't be able to protect you."

"I won't go in the nest with you, I know you're not gonna let me do that. But I'm coming to LA with you. Leave me at the hotel if you have to."

Cash squinted his eyes shut and sighed.

"I like how you decided we're getting a hotel."

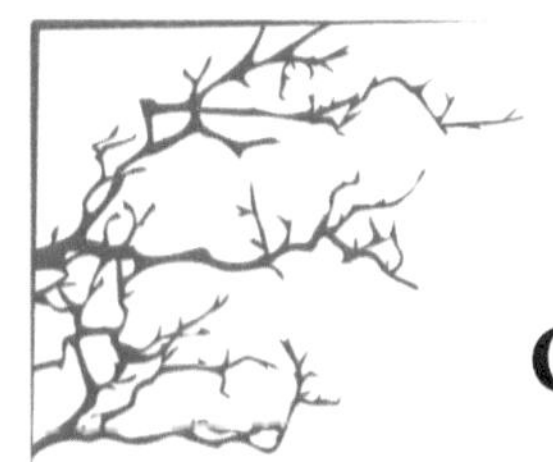

Chapter 34

As night fell Lila pushed open the concrete door of the lower crypt. She was weak from hunger but knew if she didn't bathe right away, Emil would have a field day.

The four caskets in the outer crypt remained closed. The clock, a digital clock Emil had specially programmed, read 7:45:15 PM :33 PS (post sunset). She walked past, still in the boots and leggings that she'd been in for two days.

Up the steps to the steel bulkhead door, which was easy to open from the inside but required a code on the outside. It opened into the kitchen, which overlooked the living room and loggia. The house was tastefully modern, made of concrete and glass. It was oddly

Watching for Sasha, Emil, or Cody, she went up the slat stairs to the white marble and walnut bathroom. There was something different about the house. She couldn't place it, for a moment, but then while she was showering it hit her. There was no one else here. It was just her, Sasha, Emil, and Cody. Bruce and Samson weren't here.

What could that mean? Had they defected from the nest? Emil did seem a little extra bad - perhaps they'd gotten sick of his unpredictable antics.

She dried herself and put on one of the fluffy robes folded up on the vanity. Sitting at the marble counter, she wondered what she looked like. Probably a mess despite the shower. She'd cried so much her eyes felt puffed up. And she was famished.

Lila steeled herself and went back downstairs. Whatever Emil had in mind for her, she might as well lean into it.

The curtains had been opened to reveal the floor to ceiling view of Beverly Hills below them, the red serpent of Sunset Boulevard crawling slowly through the night.

Emil and Sasha lolled across the white leather couches. It was a still night, not a ripple in the dark water of the pool. Emil was draped in a turquoise satin dressing gown. His blonde hair spiked out wildly from his head. He had one leg over the back of the couch and his head on the arm.

Sasha wore a billowing black silk maxi dress, delicate straps suspending it on her ivory shoulders. Her locks, so close to Emil's blonde that sometimes Lila thought they might be related, hung in a thick braid down her back. Her ballerina's posture draped gracefully on the overstuffed cushions.

"Please, have a seat. Now that you've managed to wash off that putrid smell."

Lila obediently deposited herself on the armchair furthest from him. He cackled.

"Ohh, she's sooo defiant." He swung his legs down and planted his bare feet on the white rug. "Are you ever so hurt that Daddy made you come home?"

Lila shrugged. Her heart was so broken it was hard to care about Emil's jabs.

"When is Cody getting here?" Sasha whined.

"Soon, my love."

Emil got up and put on the stereo. Electroclash from the early 2000s, his favorite genre. He and Sasha began to jabber over the music. Lila didn't listen.

Her thirst was growing. She hadn't eaten in several days, not since that meatball at the sports bar. Emil surely wouldn't allow her to leave the house to hunt. Perhaps he intended to simply let her starve. It wouldn't be the first time.

Around two am, Cody came home. The door from the garage swung open and he carried a young woman bridal-style into the loggia. Emil, who had been shouting about a Jodorowsky film over the thumping noise of the remixed reggaeton playing, snapped his attention first to Cody, then to Lila. She suppressed her urge to react and kept her eyes on the magazine she had found.

Cody deposited the woman on the leather cushions. She was tall and blonde, dressed in clubwear, and completely unconscious. Lila couldn't tell how old she was but she looked young. Very young.

"Ah, you brought dinner," Emil hissed, jumping up on the couch.

This poor girl, barely an adult and now through sheer bad luck a psychopath was going to drain her blood. Lila stilled her hands. There was nothing to be done for her now.

The girl made not a sound as Emil stalked across the room to her. He picked up her wrist, and let it drop.

"What did you give her, you nasty boy!" he asked Cody, not waiting to hear the answer. He knelt and pressed his mouth to the girl's neck. Seconds later blood dripped off the couch onto the floor.

Sasha waited a respectful moment, allowing her maker to fill himself up. Then she leaned over the back of the sofa and picked up the girl's wrist. Lila did not turn her face away from the bloody scene. She held still, not betraying the raging flames of thirst that boiled inside. Someday, when she was as old as Sasha, she wouldn't feel the thirst so brutally. But tonight it was so powerful her nerves were on fire holding it back.

Emil released the girl's throat and sat on the couch next to her head. His mouth was wet with red, his fangs and lips washed in it. He played with her silvery locks, letting them slip through his bloody fingers. Lila imagined the girl getting ready - curling her hair, picking an outfit. Excited to go out for the night in Hollywood.

Sitting crisscrossed, Emil stared at Lila.

"You must be terribly hungry, my pet."

Lila inclined her head, noncommittal. Sasha sat up, gore dripping off her chin. She had the blood-drunk look vampires got when they were safe and fed. The girl had gone completely pale, and the blood coming from her wrists and throat had slowed. She was close to the brink - if Cody took her to a hospital she might live.

"Wouldn't you like a taste, little baby? Isn't Baby ever so hungry?" Emil taunted.

Sasha rested her head on the back of the couch and sighed. She stretched.

"No thank you," Lila croaked.

"Are you sure?" Emil purred. He got up and moseyed across the room. One long, waxy-pale finger unfurled from his fist and tilted Lila's chin up to look at him. Lila suppressed a shudder. The fact that she had been attracted to this ghoul not six months ago blew her mind.

"I'm sure. I don't want any," she said coolly.

"Very well," he said with dramatic regret. "Sasha, you may finish her."

"No!" Lila gasped, then slapped her hand over her mouth. Emil turned to her and smirked.

"You're still so soft, my little wet nurse. We'll make you a proper monster yet," he cooed.

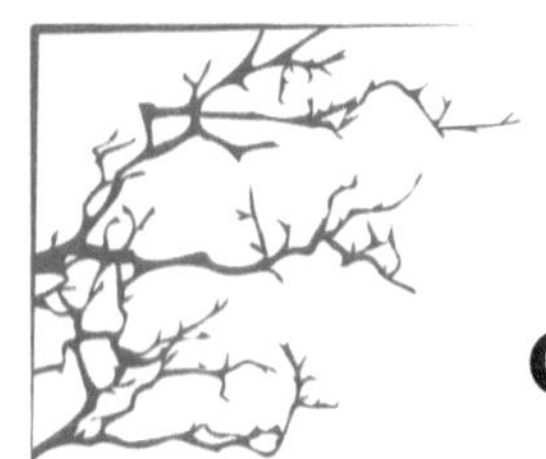

Chapter 35

Callused fingers drummed the steering wheel of Spencer's car. Cash had insisted on driving. He needed to burn off some of this energy, and he needed to think. Spencer was all too agreeable and fell asleep an hour into the five hour drive.

It was a later start than Cash had hoped for. They had eaten at Golden West, Elvis's *Aloha From Hawaii* special their musical accompaniment. Cash had downed a chocolate shake, fries, the biggest steak they had, and a side of bacon. Spencer got a grilled cheese.

Then they'd hit traffic heading east out of town, just normal commuters going home. Cash had wanted to explode. *There should be a special freeway for this,* he thought irrationally.

Now they were a few hundred miles south of Lawry on Interstate 5, pedal to the metal. Cash wanted to get a hotel sorted and start checking out the addresses they had. He thought he might know a guy in LA, too, one of Carter's friends who was in on the whole werewolf thing. If Jimmy, the friend, had any clues about where to look, all the better.

Ideally they would find the house and spend at least a few hours watching it. Cash knew that would be the most difficult part. He would want to go full wolf as soon as he saw the place.

He was not blind to the possibility that he was being delusional. For all he knew there could be thousands of vampires in Los Angeles. Lila might not even want him to find her. A million other reasons -

It didn't matter. He had to try.

"It says there's a motel on the left over there."

"On the left, or turn left?"

"Turn left."

Cash executed the turn at the last possible second before a semi barrelled through the intersection. It was eleven PM and they were in a rundown area east of Hollywood. Spencer had looked up a place to stay and navigated them from the freeway.

The motel looked clean and safe enough so Cash threw it into park.

Spencer was so tired he stumbled into the room and directly onto one of the two queen beds.

"Jeez. Like you didn't sleep all the way down, too," Cash muttered. He got undressed and brushed his teeth, but his eyes were wired open. He went out onto the walkway outside their second floor room and scented the air. It smelled horrible - metallic, chemical, human filth and waste, poverty, millions of cars. Atop those odors floated grass, Callery pear trees, jasmine, food spices. He went back inside and sat on the bed. This was all a stupid idea. His cousins - his *mom* - would never let him hear the end of it. If they ever found out.

Carolina said he was a romantic. Part of him, just a little part, had thought that when he got to LA, he would be able to follow Lila's scent straight to her. Being without her was almost painful - he was already so used to her presence, her soft body nearby, waiting to be touched. Her dry, sarcastic humor. She fit right into his life, filled a hole he didn't know the shape of. And now she was missing, only for a day, and the hole took up his entire heart.

Cash stripped the polyester motel comforter down, and stretched out atop the stiff sheets. He needed to rest, even if he couldn't sleep.

Hunger pangs wracked Lila, tearing through her body like period cramps. The three of them had come to bed some time ago. Sleep would not come for her no matter how she longed for it. She twitched in her casket, unable to get comfortable. Emil's presence was loud, the whine of a psychic car alarm. She arched her back and squirmed.

He had killed that woman - girl - right in front of her. And she had done nothing to stop it. Emil was worse than ever and Lila was afraid of how many people he would hurt to torture her. His lust for the power of blood was deranged and dangerous.

Maybe that's why Bruce and Samson weren't here. They were older than Lila, and stronger. If they left there wasn't as much Emil could do to stop them, and they had every reason to leave the nest when Emil's madness threatened to expose them. She wondered how often Cody brought victims here. Eventually the human authorities would catch up. Emil had been turned in the eighteenth century, when forensic science hadn't been invented and life was cheap. Nowadays the police could figure out where all the girls had gone. She tried to hold onto that hope, that maybe Emil would be flushed out of here by the law and she could escape him then.

She would give anything to be back in Cash's bed, those strong arms holding her. How long until she stopped missing him? Would she wonder for the rest of eternity about what they could have been?

Cold tears slipped from her eyes again. In silence, she sobbed, missing Cash's warmth and his sweetness, and *him*. He had let her be soft and scared, and he hadn't hurt her for it. She would never have that again. Emil wouldn't let her go, not ever, and every day Cash would get older and older and forget about her.

The pain of her thirst wrung through her again. She shuddered and wrapped her arms around her stomach.

She deserved this. Her history was ugly. She'd used a lot of people, even before she turned. She didn't belong with someone sweet and gentle like Cash. Not in high school and not now. She would only hurt him.

Consumed with loathing, Lila rocked side to side, letting the tears flow.

The search was not going well. Cash twitched in the passenger seat, the window down, smelling everything *but* Lila, on street after manicured street. On the corner of two leafy side streets, near a columned mansion that had been tenth on their list, he caught the most tantalizing iota of scent, maybe one part in a million. And then it evaporated in a miasma of smog and lawn chemicals.

He growled and punched the car door.

"You getting frustrated? Should we stop and eat?"

Cash checked his phone. They'd been at it for two hours.

"Yeah. Sorry, dude. This must be so boring."

"Nah. I'm just listening to this podcast."

Cash hadn't even noticed it playing. He was too focused.

Spencer punched in "burger" on his map app and flipped the car around. Cash shifted in his seat, staring ahead. He plunged his hands in his hair and shook his curls, trying to shake off the agitation.

On a shaded side street, many complicated turns away, Spencer pulled into the parking lot of Antler Burger, a cinder block stand painted white, with a red and white striped tin awning providing shade for picnic benches tucked among birds of paradise and potted palms.

Cash studied the menu and leaned down to tell the cute as a button order taker what he wanted.

"Uh, hey uh, two double Veni burgers with cheese, and a strawberry milkshake."

"You want fries with that?"

"Yeah definitely."

"And does your friend want something to drink?"

"Huh? Oh, those are both for me," Cash clarified. The girl behind the counter looked him up and down, not even being subtle.

"I like a man who can eat," she said saucily. She tapped the screen and flipped it around for Cash to dip his card. Cash turned around, tucking his card back in his wallet. Spencer was smirking at him like a cat with cream. Cash rolled his eyes. Spencer stepped up to place his order and Cash found a table.

Cash looked out at the parking lot, which sat on a corner on the uphill side of a pretty intersection, studded with cypress, elm, and jacaranda trees. The houses here were big, with sizable lots. Each one was custom, not cookie cutter floor plans like the developments he wired back home. He hadn't spent a lot of time in LA, and while he was pretty furious that his potential mate was being held captive here, the city wasn't as bad as he'd always thought. It was kind of pretty, even, in parts.

His phone buzzed. It was Carter's friend.

Hey bro. Good to hear from you, C always says he's gonna bring you around more. Anyway i don't got a line on exactly where any vamps live in BH, but look for houses w a lot of pepper trees. They plant them fuckers to throw your noses off. Fucked. Lemme know if you change your mind. I'll drop whatever to help. - grant

Pepper trees. Genius. Plant enough of those and no wolf could smell through the spice bomb.

"Here's your burgers, Baby," called the cutie pie from the order counter.

He and Spencer ate in silence. Cash assumed his customary hunched over pose, shoveling fries in his mouth, until he remembered Lila needling him about protecting his food. He straightened up.

"What are you gonna do when you find the place?" Spencer asked, wiping his mouth.

"I figure I need to sit and watch the house, like a stake out? I'm gonna wanna smash my way in but I know I can't beat full grown vampires. When Lila gets fed she's way stronger than me and she's a baby vamp."

Spencer nodded.

"So their only weaknesses are light and stakes?"

"Yeah. And they can't consume human food."

"And they're way stronger than a were?"

Cash nodded ruefully.

"My best bet is to attack during the day. First we have to find the place though."

He showed Spencer the text from Carter's friend.

"Okay. That should narrow it down. A white house with lots of pepper trees."

Getting back in the car, they headed further into Beverly Hills.

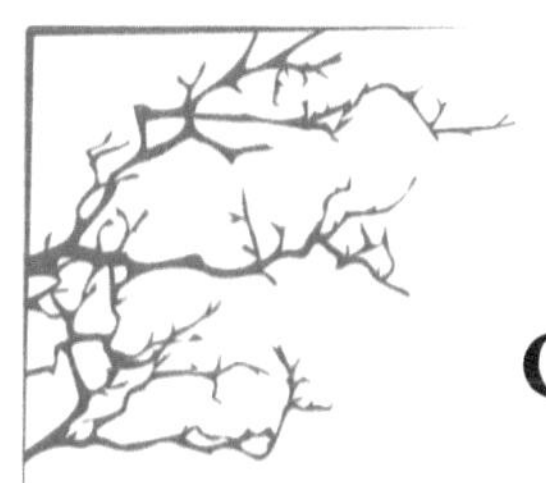

Chapter 36

Night fell without Lila having slept. Her casket sprang open, but she did not arise. She curled into a fetal ball, hoping she would be left alone to starve.

No such luck.

"Lilllaaaaaa, Princessssssaaaaa," Emil keened. He hopped up on the rim of her casket, crouching on the burgundy silk padding like a gargoyle.

"What do you want to do tonight, my pet? Shall I take you for a walk?"

Lila sighed deeply.

"Ohhh, is Baby sick? Baby needs the doctor?"

"I'm just hungry, Emil."

"Well you're in luck, then, sweetheart," he cooed. He dropped into her casket, forcing her to draw her legs up to her chest so he wouldn't land on them. He lunged forward and grabbed her wrists. With iron strength he yanked her over his shoulder and leapt out of the casket.

Emil carried Lila up to the living room and flung her on the couch. The shower was running upstairs. Cody was surely out finding a victim. In moods like this Emil was insatiable, demanding blood every night. He would feed on Cody himself if Cody failed to procure a meal.

Emil bounced from the couch to the soundsystem. He put on some dubstep and began dancing to it, dances he had learned from hunting humans at clubs.

"Cody is bringing you a special dinner, my little vegetarian."

Lila sat up.

"What does that mean?"

"Your precious morals will not be violated," he said, making finger quotes around "morals."

Lila didn't answer. She didn't dare hope. Her hunger was a steady fire in her guts, ever burning with pain.

The sun was setting. Cash was so frustrated he could explode. He sat in the driver's seat, the engine running, in the parking lot of the motel.

"Are you sure, dude?"

Spencer leaned into the open passenger window.

"Yeah. I don't need to rest. I'm gonna find them."

They said goodbye and Cash resisted peeling out on his way back to Beverly Hills. He had an idea, based on nothing, that Emil would want his nest to be up on a hill. Looking down at mortals, and with plenty of earth underneath to build his crypt.

He began to search anew, driving the switchbacks and hairpin turns of the neighborhood. He focused on addresses that, according to the satellite mapping app, were higher elevations. As he drove he looked for the telltale pepper trees.

These mansions, each unique, sat far back from the street behind walls of white stone or dense green shrubs. He could hardly see the actual building beyond many of the barriers.

All day spent driving around this place and nothing to show for it. And he'd dragged Spencer along too, like an idiot. Cash sat at a red light, fuming. His butt was tired of sitting and he longed to switch forms and run.

He thought of Lila, so soft and small, Emil's iron grip on her arm as he took her away. He had to find her, had to make sure she was okay.

The light turned green and he cranked the steering wheel, turning left up another winding hilly lane.

Something was different about this street. This hill. He felt it immediately, and it got stronger as he drove along the twisting narrow road. It wasn't quite an odor but almost an electric charge in the air. He leaned his head out of the window to sniff the air, breathing deep into his lungs. His mind raced to process all the scents, hunting out the miniscule traces that told him he was nearby.

He looked at his map app, and zoomed in on one of the red dots, double checking the street name and number.

The car crested the hill and he saw it. A flash of white stucco behind a veritable wall of pepper trees. It wasn't so different from the other mansions on this street but he knew, before he could even catch her scent, this was where Lila was.

He kept driving, past the house and down the other side of the hill a few dozen yards. He parked and considered his next move. His wolf was scratching at the door, ready to crash through the shrubbery and into the house. *Gotta be at least a little smart. As smart as I can be given how dumb this is.*

He walked in human form back up to the crest of the hill. Pretending to look at his phone, he watched the house from a distance of twenty yards. He listened, straining to hear anything from within. It was still so quiet - maybe they hadn't risen yet? The whole street was oddly quiet.

A few yards closer, until he was at the wall of pepper trees, peering through. The scent was overwhelming and blotted out all others, threatening to set him sneezing until Cash tucked his nose under his shirt collar to filter it out a bit. Behind the foliage lay a perfectly manicured lawn, leading up to a wall of towering juniper trees. Two tree walls, both heavily scented. This guy really did not want any werewolves to find him.

There was a short chain link fence hidden among the pepper trees. Cash jumped it, landing lightly on the fallen leaves and peppercorns on the other side. He crouched down and waited, watching the lawn. Maybe Emil was rich enough to have private security patrolling the grounds. There were no signs of electronic security, no security company stickers or camera lenses winking from the hedges.

Moving fast and silent he traversed the lawn to the second hedge, the junipers.

When he peaked through these, his breath caught. This was it. It had to be.

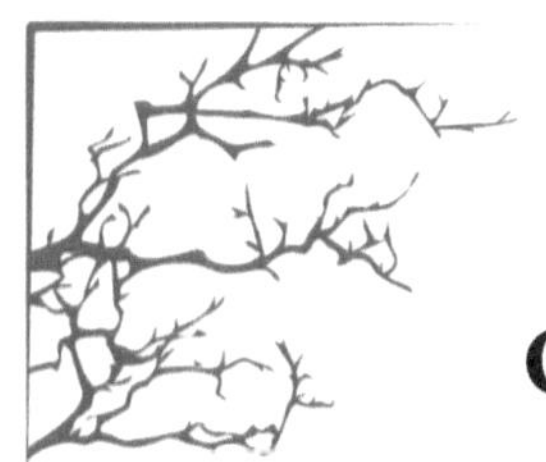

Chapter 37

A rectangular pool, surrounded by a patio and loggia divided from the house by a wall of glass. The house was big, white, modern. He had approached it from behind - the entrance must be on the street below. As he watched, black curtains began to rise, revealing an angular modern room divided from the patio by the glass wall. Lights came on inside, revealing the details of the interior. The house was a U shape, the living room being in the cradle of the U. There was a second story with a balcony overlooking the room. He compared it to a courtyard, but enclosed. Perhaps so it could be light proofed. The bottom half of the glass wall consisted of door panels, and those too opened as if automatically, rotating until perpendicular with the wall.

Cash waited but no one appeared. He glanced around behind him, then slid along the trees until he was as close as he could get to the patio without stepping away from the trees and their shadows.

The lack of security was shocking. Maybe Emil was so arrogant he thought he didn't need it. Maybe he actually didn't need it, and Cash was the one being arrogant by challenging a den of vampires.

He distracted himself by studying the layout of the room. A half-wall to the left divided the massive entertaining kitchen from the living room. To the right, stairs leading up to the second storey. The house was large but not as palatial as he expected. He had worked on homes like this one, the Silicon Valley version. How had Emil come by a mansion, anyway? Lucky investments? Murder?

The decor was so white-dominant that Cash began to doubt he was in the right place. Surely vampires would be concerned about blood stains? Shit, if he had just trespassed on some white person's mansion he was going to get himself shot.

But then the wind shifted and he was hit with the scent of dead blood. Much more than a trace - a facefull of the odor, metallic and oddly fatty. And then, a tendril of Lila's dead flower essence. He was in the right place and she was here, right now.

He stilled himself. The urge to transform, to barge into the house, was a klaxon in his head. But he had planned to gather recon first, to at least attempt to have a good idea what he was getting into. He had to wait.

He waited, every muscle tense. Adrenaline coursed through his veins, spurring the wolf in him to emerge, but he took a deep breath and forced it down. He needed to be clear. Breathing that intense blood smell was helping - it wasn't exactly nauseating but it was so strange that his wolfy mind wanted to puzzle over it. The breeze ruffled his hair in the unbearable stillness.

He didn't have to wait long. The vampire he figured had to be Sasha emerged from cellar doors into the open area, letting the doors crash into the walls next to them. Sasha was tall and angular, with long blonde hair. She had on a floor length white satin dressing gown - like a vampire in a movie. Cash watched her stalk across the living room and up the curving glass stairs to the upper level, and disappear behind a door. From up there you'd be able to see across half of LA. Just as he'd thought - Emil had chosen a nest he could look down on mortals from.

Shortly after Sasha had gone upstairs, Emil arose from the basement, with Lila over his shoulder. Cash's heart lurched at the sight of her hanging over Emil like a ragdoll. Then Emil dumped her onto the sofa, and Cash had to bite into his wrist to keep from running straight into the house and attacking. Lila looked emaciated - her skin was gray and her eyes were hollow. She lay on the cushions limp, her black hair splayed around her head like a broken halo.

Cash couldn't suppress a growl. He couldn't keep his wolf in, either. Gold took his eyes and his teeth and ears sprang out.

He crept closer to the house, until he was at the very edge of the junipers' shadows. If Emil or Lila looked in this direction they would easily see him, but he was pretty sure he wouldn't be noticed if he held still.

Emil moved around the room like a satyr on PCP, putting on music and dancing unrhythmically. A look of manic jubilation sat on his face like a mask. Rage boiled inside, pushing his claws out.

He breathed deep, scenting the air. There was Lila's scent, and another that must be Emil. A trace of a third - Sasha. He couldn't smell the other two Lila had mentioned, Samson and Bruce. Nor could he smell the human who had been with Emil before, in Lawry.

Lila moved. He zeroed in on her. She shifted, curling into a ball on her side, her cheek on a throw pillow. It seemed she might fall asleep, but then her eyes snapped open and flew to his.

His heart pounded. She could see him. Her eyes went wide and she shook her head almost imperceptibly. Cash shook his back, refusing her signal to leave. He was so close now. He had to wait for the right moment. Whether he simply grabbed Lila and ran or attacked Emil head on remained to be seen.

Lila sat up. Her dark head lolled back, resting on the cushion behind her. Emil did a serpentine dance, his silky kaftan floating around him. There was a violent grace to him, like a fencer. He was light on his feet and unpredictable.

The unmistakable sound of a garage door going up. Emil spun towards the entryway, separated from the atrium-like living room by a short staircase, and clapped his hands gleefully.

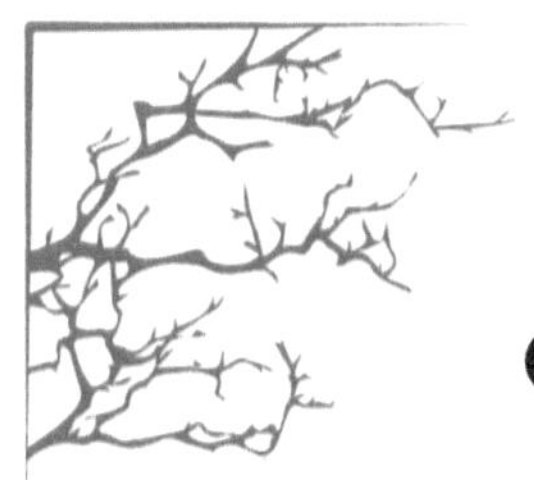

Chapter 38

Emil leapt, goblinesque, onto the couch, framing Lila between his legs. Cash's fists contracted. Emil crouched down and whispered something in Lila's ear. Her head rolled away from his listlessly. He flipped his irregular blonde hair up off his face and jumped over the couch. He began to prance towards the entryway and Cash crept forward another foot, closer and closer to the edge of the patio's paving.

Emil bounded back into his line of sight, the human henchman in tow.

The human man carried a sack of blood. An IV bag for a transfusion. He held it like an old-timey robber would hold a money sack with a big dollar sign on the front. The thick red liquid sloshed around in the translucent plastic. Emil jigged next to the lumbering hulk. Good lord, he was tiresome. Like a jittery marionette.

"Little vegetarian, are you hungry?"

Lila lifted her head. Her dark eyes followed the bag of blood as Emil brought it to her. Upstairs, the shower shut off. Sasha emerged and leaned over the rail on the upstairs landing, watching. Cash shrank back, hoping to remain out of her eye line. Her expression was bored, and she gazed upon the proceedings as indifferent as the Sphinx.

If he could just get closer. Lila was only a dozen yards away. She sat upright, strain tensing her posture. She would be close to feral now - she hadn't fed since Sunday. Emil swung the IV bag in front of her face.

"Yes, you're terribly hungry, aren't you little lamb?"

Cash watched Lila nod in resignation. Emil held the bag above her and pricked a hole in the thick plastic with his pinky nail. Lila stuck her mouth under the stream of gore, lapping it up. She swallowed greedily and blood splattered her lips and chest.

Strange, thought Cash. Wasn't Emil hungry? His jerky, unpredictable movement had Cash wondering if vampires could do drugs, if maybe Emil was on vampire cocaine and therefore had no appetite.

The strange little blonde jester danced to the music, his spikes of hair bobbing to the beat. Lila stood up from the couch and took a step towards the glass wall. Her eyes were wide and dark, and she clutched at her stomach. For a moment, her eyes lit up, and the rage he saw in her face gave him hope that she wasn't as weakened as he'd thought.

Then she bent double and began to heave up streams of red.

"Oh, did I forget to mention? It's horse blood. Since I know you would never take a *human* life," Emil sneered.

Lila convulsed, a waterfall of blood pouring out of her nose and mouth, splashing on the white couch and rug. She collapsed onto the white rug, red spreading around her as she seized.

The sight of her crumpling triggered Cash's inner wolf, and before he had anything to say about it, the change was rippling over him, his muscles stretching and fur sprouting all over his body. His jeans and shirt shredded apart as his body grew.

He shook himself, then took a running start. He hurtled through the closest open door and snatched Emil up by the waist. Capitalizing on Emil's surprise, Cash threw the vampire sire through the plate glass wall. It shattered, raining glass down. Cash lept to Lila's side and cradled her head in his lap.

She looked up at him, thick black blood streaming from her nose and eyes. Her eyes wouldn't focus on him. The light in them was fading.

The henchman rushed Cash, but Cash saw it from a mile away and wheeled on Cody, slashing across his face and throat with his claws. Cody stumbled backward, his face gushing.

Sasha, apparently starving herself, was there in a flash, her mouth on Cody's wound. Cash turned back to Lila.

"I'm gonna feed you," he said, desperate to help her somehow. She convulsed in his lap. "Stay with me, Lila. You're gonna be okay."

He lifted his wrist to her fangs. She hesitated.

"It's okay. You won't hurt me. Do it. You'll die," he murmured. He would say anything to get her to drink. With effort, she lifted her head and sank her teeth into his wrist. Her eyes drifted closed and she began to feed.

"You stupid fucking stray dog. I'm going to shred you," Emil screamed, dragging himself up from the shattered glass. Dozens of cuts mutilated him, and his black blood poured from his face. As Cash watched they began to seal up, and then he turned his eyes on Cash. They were red as the dawn and filled with rage. He bared his teeth, and sprinted towards them.

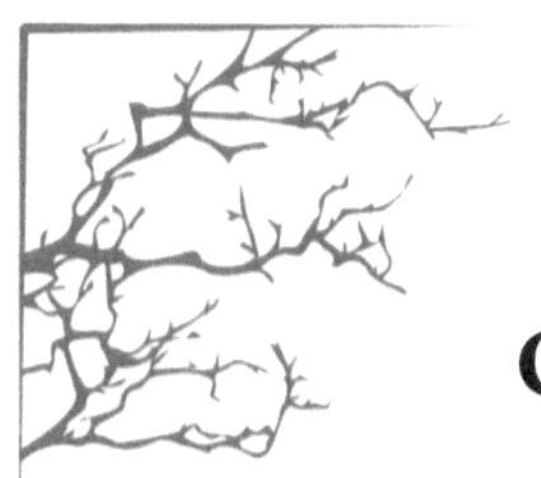

Chapter 39

The equine blood had been boiling acid, burning on its way out of her. It leaked from her eyes and nose as her stomach cramped up. She would be sick for days.

Or she would have if Cash hadn't come. He had come here for her. He had found her somehow? She was so confused. He had fed her from his wrist, and now the acid pain was replaced with a sensation of power unlike anything she had felt before.

Cash's magic wolf blood filled her, forcing the poisonous animal blood out. It was like being filled with golden light, with electricity. Was she beginning to actually glow?

Then she felt him ripped away from her. Her eyes flew open in time to see Emil throw Cash across the room. He hit the glass staircase, his back hitting the steps with a sickening crunch.

Emil advanced towards him.

She leapt to her feet.

"Emil!" she bellowed, and began to run at him. Faster than she knew she was capable of.

"No!" Sasha shouted, rushing her from the side. Lila pivoted at the last second, throwing Sasha off balance. She swept the blonde's legs out from under her, letting Sasha hit the marble floor. Lila fell on her and slashed her throat with a ferocity that was brand new, and felt like lightning in her veins.

Sasha's black blood geysered out of her and splashed all over Lila.

She dragged herself up and left Sasha to clutch at her neck. *She'll be fine*, Lila thought bitterly. *After all, she just fed.*

She turned on Emil, who had reached Cash and the glass staircase. Emil stood above Cash's motionless body.

"You motherfucker! If you killed him I will tear you apart!" She didn't recognize her own voice. It was a howl, a banshee's wail.

Emil sneered back at her.

"You could try," he hissed.

In a flash Lila was on him. She grabbed him by the hair and yanked backwards. To her shock his scalp ripped off entirely.

"Gross!" she shouted, throwing it across the room. He stumbled at her, his robe soaking up his own blood. She punched him, connecting with first his nose then his lip. His betrayed, furious expression almost made her laugh. She grabbed his throat, her claws sinking into the skin to either side of his windpipe. With her other arm she pinned his to her side. Emil looked down at her, his eyes ablaze.

"You have no idea what you're doing," he snapped.

"Cash!" Lila cried, her eyes not leaving Emil's. "Are you alive?"

Cash groaned.

"Maybe I should tear you apart anyway," Lila murmured. She licked her teeth. She'd never been so powerful before. "You lied to me. This isn't a double curse."

"You little fool. You're not immortal anymore. That animal has ruined your gift."

Lila almost spat in his face.

"I never wanted this gift." Her eyes narrowed. "Let me go. Don't come after me."

"Come after you?" he snarled. "If you ever come back to LA I'll make you wish you'd never been born."

"Way ahead of you," she snapped. She released his arm and his hand flew to his scalp, which was already beginning to reform. "We're leaving now." Her other hand dropped and she went to Cash's side.

"Can you walk?" she asked tenderly, kneeling on the step next to him. His shoulder hung at an unnatural angle, and his wolfiness was receding gradually, leaving his bruised and naked human form in its wake. Lila lifted him, putting his good arm over her shoulders.

Once he was upright he could mostly support himself. She held onto his elbow to make sure he didn't slip on the many puddles of blood. She spared another glance at Emil. Blazing wrath etched his features into a grimace. She snarled, her lips lifting in a lupine expression of fury.

Cash pointed up the lawn, towards the street at the rear of the lot. As they passed through the pepper trees and over the fence, Sasha's scream rose behind them.

"FUCKING CUNT!"

Cash looked down at her and Lila couldn't help it. She burst out laughing.

Lila could not - would not - let go of Cash's hand as they left the mansion and walked up the hill towards the car. They were both splattered with blood and Cash was naked. By some miracle no one drove past.

Cash popped the trunk and pulled out two wool plush blankets. He handed one to Lila.

"Spencer's car. He always keeps blankies in the trunk," Cash explained. She took it gratefully and wrapped it around herself, using one corner to wipe the blood off her face. He pulled her tightly to him. A happy little squeak came out of her and he melted for her, again.

"I'm so glad you're okay," he murmured. She rested her ear on his chest and relaxed into him, rearranging her blanket so she could reach under his and squeeze him back.

"I'm glad you are too." She looked up at him through big hazel eyes that flashed gold, just like a werewolf. "Thank you for coming all this way to save me."

He looked down at her, his biceps flexing to pull her even tighter.

"I would have gone anywhere," he said.

"You fed me," she said dreamily. His blood still raced in her veins, burning with life and energy. She licked her lips, her fangs gleaming. "I would have died but you fed me."

"I didn't know if it would work," Cash said ruefully. "We got lucky."

"I don't think it was luck. I think you knew subconsciously that Emil is full of shit about everything he told me."

Cash snorted. They stilled, gazing at each other.

"Can I touch your hair?" she asked him. He nodded. They should get going, but he was naked and Lila was pressing her lithe, soft body to his.

She reached her arms up to clasp them around his neck, her hands sinking into his curls.

"I missed you," he murmured.

She tilted her head up to his, and he met her lips, his tongue lapping at her fangs. She opened for him, kissing him back. His hands tightened on her back.

Heat built between them, and Cash broke away to slow his racing heart. Lila threw her head back, baring her throat to him, and then lowered her chin to look at him. She sighed deeply and bit her lip.

"I missed you too," She tucked her blanket around her. He opened the passenger side and helped her in, then got behind the wheel.

When they got back to the motel, it was one AM. But Spencer was awake and red-eyed when he let them into the room.

"Dude! You're okay!" he exclaimed, dragging Cash into a hug. "And YOU'RE okay!" he said to Lila. He hesitated before hugging her, but she practically jumped to hug him.

"Spencer! You're here," she said.

"Hey! Yeah! You all good?" he asked.

"I've literally never felt more alive," she answered, grinning. Spencer's face split into his choirboy grin, dimples an dall.

The three of them sat down on the two beds. Neither of them had been slept in. Spencer had waited up. Cash felt a flood of affection for his best friend.

"So what happened? How'd you get out of there?"

"Seems like I'm part werewolf now," Lila said. Spencer's brows shot up.

"Like part vamp part wolf? How does that work?"
Lila shrugged.

"I guess we'll find out."

Cash stood up, clutching the blanket around his waist.

"We need a second room," he announced.

"Oh yeah. I'll go sort that out with the front desk," Spencer said, rising as well. He popped out and Lila and Cash were alone again. Cash began to gather his overnight bag.

"Cash," Lila said, and he paused and looked at her. "Thank you."

He shrugged and made a noncommittal sound.

"No. You didn't need to do any of this. You saved my life."

She stood up and moved to him.

"You saved me," she repeated, looking up at him.

Instead of answering, he took her face in his hand and tipped it up to his. His lips brushed hers gently.

"I had to," he answered. His eyes searched hers. "I couldn't let you go."

She flung her arms around his neck and pressed herself to him. He hugged her tight to him, stroking her damp hair, and she rested her cheek on his chest.

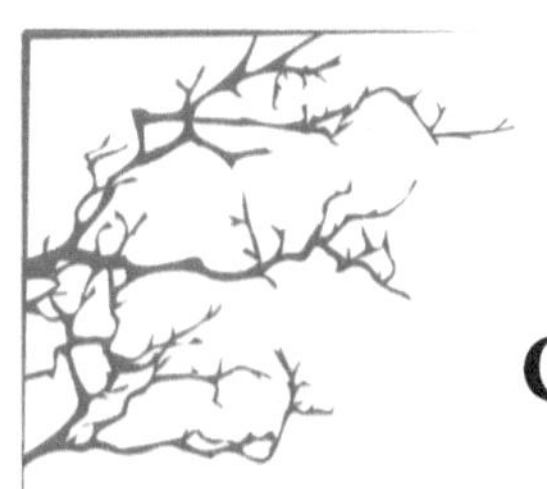

Chapter 40

With an hour or so to spare until dawn, Lila and Cash finished light proofing the second motel room. Duct tape sealed the window and door, and the room was dark enough for Lila to feel safe.

She showered first. The stench of Sasha's blood, of her own blood vomit, washed down the drain.

While Cash took over the bathroom, she hung her towel over a chair and helped herself to one of his undershirts to sleep in. She slipped her clean body between the cool, stiff sheets. The sensations helped ground her against the fever inside. Jittery energy, the afterglow from chugging electrified werewolf blood, coursed through her in adrenaline waves.

Eyes closed, she rolled over to her side to face the middle. Flashes of the confrontation earlier greeted her. Her hunger, so fierce it was a possession. The foul animal blood that burned as her body rejected it, and then the weakness and... and vertigo. Like sinking face-up into a never ending well. Death seemed to come again, as it had when she had turned. Only this was the eternal death.

Acceptance had washed over her. Her life had been shit. And now it was truly over. And then the golden, honey-thick, rich blood began to flow between her lips. She smelled Cash, tasted him, all throughout her body at once, and her nerves sang in answer to his life energy.

And then he was ripped from her and she sprang to life, stronger than ever.

It hadn't sunk in that she was free. She didn't have to hide from Emil anymore. Once they left tonight, she never had to see him again.

And she and Cash could be together, without it risking his life. It was too much at once - there had to be a catch.

The sound of the shower reminded her that Cash was here, had come here to get her. He put himself up against full grown vampires - and he had no way of knowing there were only two. It made her heart thud painfully in her chest. He wouldn't do that if he didn't care for her. People didn't do that just to make up for a favor you did in ninth grade.

She thought of how he had cuddled her to sleep, his chest warming her, his arms wrapped protectively around her. The memory brought her a wave of comfort, and she closed her eyes.

Cash ran cheap motel conditioner through his curls. Pink lather ran down his body as the blood came out of his hair. He was sore and tired. His shoulder had healed but it would be achy for a few days. Despite the general shittiness of this motel the water pressure was intense, and it pounded some of the tension out of his shoulders.

Lila was going to be okay. She was free. She had tried his blood and it didn't hurt her. He shouldn't get ahead of himself. But the barriers that stood between them were dropping away. He had some small glimmer of hope that they might be able to make something together. A life. A pack.

"I'm wrung the fuck-" Cash started to say as he left the bathroom, fresh as a daisy in clean boxer briefs. He shut up when he saw Lila, asleep under just the sheet. Her face was more serene than he had ever seen it, even the eleven between her brows smoothed away.

Her little fangs poked through as she sighed in her sleep.

Cash would have fought a million vampires to save her. He didn't give a shit what Carter or anyone said. Maybe she would break his heart. It would be worth it to find out.

He eased himself down on the bed, doing his best not to disturb her.

"Cash," she whispered. Without opening her eyes, she rolled over and scooted close so her soft, supple ass was flush with his package. Then she pressed her back into his chest and pulled his arm over her like a blanket.

He chuckled and kissed the top of her head, and settled in. If he had been any less exhausted, the temptation to wake her up with his mouth would have been hard to resist. As it was, his limbs were lead, and he sank into the mattress, wrapped around his vampire baby.

Lila woke slowly as the sun set the next evening. Cash was wrapped around her, his arms surrounding her and their legs tangled. Delicious heat and comfort radiated from his body, so she snuggled deeper into him.

Mmm, hello, she thought as she felt him lengthening against the round of her ass. *Is he awake at all?*

She stopped wiggling her butt against his hard on, and twisted up to nuzzle her face to his neck and chin. A grumbly sound, and he nuzzled her in return. She giggled when his stubble tickled her neck and he opened his eyes.

"You're really here," he rumbled, his voice extra deep from sleep.

"Of course I am," she said. He smiled sleepily and kissed her, hard, holding her chin between his thumb and forefinger. His other arm, underneath her, pulled her even tighter to him.

"Good morning," he said. He let go of her chin and buried his face in her neck, and rocked his hips into her ass. She moaned softly in encouragement.

He lifted his head to meet her eyes.

"Thank you for coming for me," she blurted. She was looking at him with an expression so tender and sweet, his heart flipped over.

"You don't have to thank me," he answered, bending to kiss her neck.

"I was ready to give up."

The thought of Lila acquiescing to that nightmare clown made him ill.

"No one can ever make you do that again," he replied, tightening his arm around her. "You have me to feed on now."

"What?"

"You can just feed on me," he explained. "If... if you want."

Lila blinked. She hadn't even considered that Cash might be willing to feed her again. It had been an emergency act.

"You don't... you don't have to do that. You've already done so much for me."

"I want to," he said, not missing a heartbeat. "To be totally honest... it's kind of hot."

Lila gasped, shocked by how much that statement turned her on. Cash buried his face in her neck again.

He nipped and kissed at her neck, not touching her body, until she arched her back and whined. Her nipples stood up under her white tank top, and he brushed them lightly, making her shiver.

She reached behind her and clasped his erection where it strained the cotton of his undies. He flipped the sheet off and kissed her again, licking into her mouth. Lila shifted so she was on her back. She stroked him and he sought out the apex of her thighs. Her knees parted for his big hand and he circled her clit, lightly, gathering her juices on his fingertips. He leaned down and took her soft flesh in his mouth through her tank top, the wet heat enveloping her pert nipple. She pushed his hair off his neck and kissed the tender skin of his shoulder, the only part of him she could reach.

"Do you wanna feed right now?" he murmured into her breast.

"Yes," she gasped.

"Fuck, you just got so much wetter," he said, his voice going even deeper.

"Can I?" she asked.

"Of course," he answered. He moved to bring his carotid artery closer to her mouth. She shuddered with anticipation, and lifted her lip to unsheath her fangs.

Cash swirled his fingers in her wetness. Lila nicked his velvety skin, and he growled. Hot salty blood spilled into her hungry mouth. She lapped at his skin, drinking him down, the heat and power of him coursing through her. She moaned into his neck and he slipped his middle finger into her. He ground his hard length into her hip.

Lila slipped her hand under his waistband. She ran her fingers through his silky precum and all over his swollen head. Her need for him was undeniable, aching in her like hunger.

She spread her knees wider and he dipped another finger into her, his mouth never stilling on her breast. His life force filled her, pleasure filled her, spreading through her veins like morphine.

She let out a choked cry as another digit slipped into her, and then back out just as quickly. He returned to her clit, dancing over the swollen bud nimbly.

She licked at his blood, gorging herself. She forced herself to release his throat. She licked her lips greedily, and pulled his head up to kiss her. He groaned into her mouth, tasting his own blood on her tongue.

Lila began to pant, the tension winding up in her already. Cash already knew her body after just once together, and he was taking her apart without breaking a sweat. She was so aroused, her cunt throbbing with need.

He dipped his long fingers in and out of her, teasing out her climax, until she wanted to beg. He spread her puffy lips open to expose more of her nerves to his expert fingers. She cried out, the tension snapping, and curled around his hand as she came. Shockwaves of pleasure, enhanced by the feeding, burst through her body.

His touch slowed as she began to descend. Without speaking, he tugged his boxer briefs off. Freed, his cock lay hot and heavy across her middle. He took her chin again, and kissed her. His hand moved to rest on her throat, and she was helpless, boneless, in his arms.

Cash reached down to position himself at her entrance. He lifted her leg over his hip, reaching her from behind and below. The position kept her spread wide for him and his hand free to explore her.

"I want you now," he whispered in her ear. His hot breath on her neck was enough to stand her nerves on end again.

"God yes," she sighed, and he nudged into her.

They both stilled. Lila's inner walls fluttered wildly with aftershocks. Cash needed a moment to get control of himself. Feeling her feed on him had driven the wolf in him into a frenzy. He was on the verge of losing it completely in her.

He eased in, inch by inch, until his hips were flush with hers. Her eyes were closed and she had her bottom lip between her teeth, her perfect bloodstained fangs making two tiny dents in the rosy skin. Cash slid his hand back to rest at her throat. Her hand met his, stroking his fingers in a silent assent. Lila rocked her hips in case he still wasn't sure, and Cash began to move, thrusting slowly at first.

Her face began to screw up as another orgasm built. Cash was sure he would never be sick of this sight, of the little eleven that formed between her brows as she chased her pleasure. His hand left her throat and moved to rub little circles on her clit. He was greedy. He wanted to see her fall apart again, wanted to feel her squeezing him.

He didn't have to wait long. Lila's breathy, throaty cries grew faster and louder, and then she was spasming around him, chanting his name as her hot silky walls throttled his cock. He thrust harder, faster, giving her more and more. She wrapped her arms around his neck and kissed him and he came, spilling in her, burying his face in her neck.

Cash collapsed half on top of Lila, breathing hard. She drew lazy figure eights on his back.

"Hold still," he said, getting up to fetch a warm damp towel. When he came back, Lila hadn't moved a muscle.

"You good?" he chuckled as he cleaned her up.

"So good," she answered, flopping her arm over her face theatrically. Cash grinned. He chucked the towel into the bathroom and climbed onto the bed, caging her under him. He bent to kiss her, letting his tongue trace her fangs. Their little points scraping his flesh sent a zipline of goosebumps up his back.

He silently pledged to feed her every day. The way it had made him feel, he knew he would be hooked on that forever. Feeding her, providing for her, that was just part of it. The way she lit up, her eyes aglow, she didn't have that when she fed on humans. If he had his way she would never drink from a human again - why miss out on the feral goddess she became when he fed her?

"Five more minutes," she murmured, as he settled back down next to her.

"I'll hit the snooze button for you, Killer."

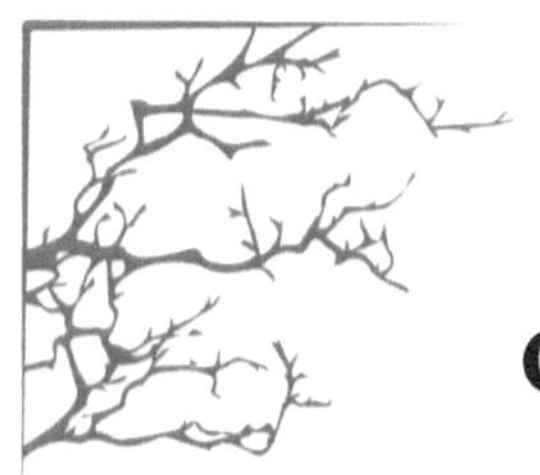

Chapter 41

Lila signed out of her online art course and closed her laptop. Tonight was the full moon, and Cash would be home from work soon.

She stretched and got up off the bed. The bedroom they shared was still light proofed with blankets, but Cash had gotten the wood to build blackout shutters for all the windows. They planned to install it all this weekend.

Not tonight though. It was date night.

Black denim shorts, one of Cash's old Slayer tee shirts, and... engineer boots. She pulled the outfit out of her side of the closet and changed out of her leggings and sports bra.

As she was putting on mascara she heard his truck outside and checked the time.

"You up, babe?" he called from the front door. "Sun's almost down."

He came into the bedroom.

"Hey Killer," he growled, sliding his arms around her waist and lifting her. She wrapped her legs around his middle and took his face in her hands.

Their lips met in a kiss that started out sweet but heated up immediately, until Cash's hands were moving down to Lila's ass and she was arching into him.

"How was your day?" she asked dreamily when they came up for air. He set her down and began taking off his work boots.

"Oh, you know Nilo, always on someone about something. You hungry?"

She shook her head.

"Let me do your hair later. When we get back," she said, sitting next to him and winding one of his curls around her finger.

"Really? It's not a pain?"

"No! I like it." When Cash washed his hair, Lila sat on the couch behind him and serenely detangled his mane, running curl balm through each section until Cash was melty and purring. It was her favorite part of the week.

Cash's favorite part of the week was when Lila fed on him. The way it turned her wild made him want to put a ring on her finger.

"I'm gonna eat a burrito," he said, changing from his black work jeans to a clean pair of black jeans. He pulled his work shirt off and Lila unabashedly admired him, running her eyes down his body from his collarbone to his Adonis belt and treasure trail.

"The sun's pretty much down?" she confirmed, getting up.

"Yeah you're good."

His blood had given her a much higher tolerance for light. She still couldn't be in the daylight, but the full moon no longer weakened her.

While Cash ate, they shared their days. Lila had learned about the Dada movement and Cash had started wiring a tech billionaire's new house.

Cash put his plate in the dishwasher and got a beer.

Lila sat at the kitchen island, drumming her fingers impatiently.

Cash chuckled.

"You wanna go pretty bad, huh?"

She nodded.

"The sooner we meet Spencer and Carolina, the sooner we can go run," she reasoned.

"You wanna watch me change?"

She nodded again, her lower lip going between her teeth. His eyes darkened. She thought his beast form was... sexy. He wasn't going to question it. He drained his beer

"Vamanos, Killer," he said, sticking out his elbow for her to take. She let him lead her out to the truck.

Tonight he would transform into his half-wolf, so he could talk to Lila as they ran through the woods together. He loved watching her spectral form racing through the forest, agile as a puma.

First though, they were having drinks with Spencer, Melissa, and Carolina at El Greco. Spencer had practically had kittens when he found out Lila had never set foot inside.

"What, that creepy red place downtown? No, I left way before I turned twenty one."

"Oh my GOD. We're going. This Friday. It's on."

Now it was this Friday. Cash eased the truck into the parking lot and came around to open Lila's door.

"Holy shit. This place is wild," she exclaimed, taking in the elaborate decor. Cash spotted their friends in a booth in the corner.

"Anybody need a drink?" he asked after they'd said hello.

"I'll go with you," Carolina offered. She got up. Lila sat down in her place.

"Laphroaig for you Cash?"

"Just a Bud tonight, Bon."

The Scotch would only dull his urge to shift, and he wanted to feel it fully later.

"I can admit when I'm wrong." Carolina turned to him, after Bonnie went to get their beers.

"Aw, come on Caro. It's not that you were wrong," Cash demurred, shaking his head.

"Well I feel like an asshole."

"You're not. I would have said the same thing."

"Are you sure you're not mad?"

"You'd have to do a lot more than that to make me mad at you," Cash promised. "Anyway, you're coming with us to the desert next week right?"

"Yeah. For sure. You know I wouldn't miss a chance to ogle Carter in person."

"I don't know why we have family reunions so often. I think Mom organized this one just to give Lila the once over."

"You love it though. And they're gonna love her."

He grinned and caught Carolina's shoulders in a tight side hug.

As much as Lila liked El Greco and hanging out with Cash's friends, she was antsy as hell to go run in the woods with him. She loved seeing his animal form, the grace with which he bounded through the forest in the silver light. After what felt like an eternity, they said their goodbyes and she hustled him into the truck.

She drove, speeding down the backroads, her night vision now only slightly impaired by the headlights. Her hand found Cash's across the console.

Not quickly enough, they reached the trail head. Cash wasted no time in stripping off his jeans and shoes.

With a deep growl, he let the wild wash over him, and his muscles and bones began to shift and stretch. Long hooked claws sprang from his fingers as fangs tore out of his jaws. He grew taller, and fur rippled from his neck down to his paws and tail. His eyes glowed yellow, and his transformation was complete.

Enraptured, Lila came to him and stood on her tiptoes to kiss his monstrous face. His chest rumbled and his arms circled possessively around her.

"Let's run, baby," she whispered. His clawed paw came up to caress her cheek, then dropped to clasp her hand, enclosing it in his furry fist. Cash threw his head back and howled, and together they took off, running in the moonlight.

Acknowledgements

My deepest gratitude to my husband, Matt Howse; my parents, Jack and Rose Barry; my besties Ann, Erika, Justine, and Barb for keeping me going; my beta reader Bridget Salvia; brilliant cover artist and friend Bud Sypeck; and all the good buddies of Discussion Group.

About the Author

Luxe Huntley is the pen name of Brigid Howse.

Brigid has been fascinated with monsters since she was a small spooky child. She has been writing about them almost as long.

Brigid lives in Southern California with her husband and many chihuahuas

Read more at https://www.luxehuntley.com/.